Zarathustra Must Die

Zarathustra Must Die

DORIAN ALEXANDER

etruscan press

Etruscan Press
Wilkes University
84 West South Street
Wilkes-Barre, PA 18766

WILKES UNIVERSITY

www.etruscanpress.org

Published 2012 by Etruscan Press
Printed in the United States of America
Design by Julianne Popovec
The text of this book is set in Adobe Caslon Pro.

First Edition
12 13 14 15 16 5 4 3 2 1

Library of Congress Cataloging-in-Publication Data

Alexander, Dorian.
  Zarathustra must die / Dorian Alexander.
    p. cm.
  ISBN 978-0-9832944-4-3 (pbk.)
  1. Graduate students--Fiction. 2. Time--Fiction. 3. Nietzsche, Friedrich
Wilhelm, 1844-1900--Fiction. I. Title.
  PS3601.L35375Z37 2012
  813'.6--dc23

Please turn to the back of this book for a list of the sustaining funders of Etruscan
Press.

For believe me: the secret for harvesting from existence the greatest fruitfulness and the greatest enjoyment is—to live dangerously! Build your cities on the slopes of Vesuvius!

—Friedrich Nietzsche

Zarathustra Must Die

Zarathustra
Must Die

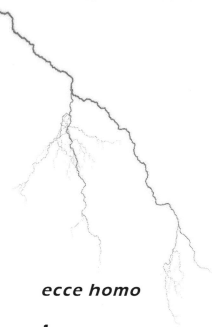

ecce homo

1.

Nietzsche went insane. One year after writing penetrating albeit grandiose works, Friedrich Wilhelm Nietzsche went completely and utterly insane. His friend Franz Overbeck found him trembling in Turin, cowering on the ground, rising up, giving violent embraces, and crouching down again to whisper the revelation that he himself had replaced the dead God. Nietzsche, the Dionysus and the Crucified One, hung on the neck of a horse to stop a flogging, then fell to the streets of Turin, crushed by the weight of the cross he was bearing. Even in madness, Nietzsche was a master of the return. The good European was taken from his last home in Italy and returned to Basel, Switzerland, where at the remarkable age of twenty-four he had once been appointed professor of philology. From there he was taken to Jena for further treatment and then returned to his childhood home in Naumberg, Germany, where he had lived from the age of five after the death of his father. How did this clairvoyant fall into darkness? Always a sickly

3

man with a weak belly and poor eyesight, did even this visionary have trouble stomaching the twilight of the nineteenth century? He tried to raise the sun, tried to usher in a new dawn in an age when others were too blind to see that night was falling. Nietzsche was a philosopher of the future, who retreated to the past, in order to discover the eternal recurrence of the present.

Nietzsche died in 1900, at the birth of a century in which he would be reborn as both icon and iconoclast. He left us with many great works, among them his own intellectual autobiography. Written in 1888, the year before he went mad, the book was modestly entitled *Ecce Homo*. A Latin phrase meaning "behold the man," the title might pass unnoticed for an autobiography had it not been uttered by Pontius Pilate when he presented Christ to the masses. This is not surprising, as Nietzsche had already made it quite clear that he intended to supplant Christ as the central figure of Western culture. The four chapter titles reflect a commensurate humility: "Why I Am So Wise," "Why I Am So Clever," "Why I Write Such Good Books," and "Why I Am a Destiny." In retrospect, I cannot condemn them as hyperbolic, as Nietzsche was, indeed, wise, clever—and a destiny. What knits my brow is the curious subtitle of the book: *How One Becomes What One Is*. What could this mean? Why and how do I become what I already am? And what am I, then, if I *cannot* become it?

2.

On further reflection, I suppose the subtitle makes some sense considering the history of nineteenth century philosophy in Continental Europe. The century was dominated in many respects by the comprehensive intellectual masterpieces of Georg F.W. Hegel, as well as by his followers and detractors. Hegel had a cosmic schema of the Idea unfolding dialectically over time toward Freedom. However, this highly systematic schema was rejected by the Danish philosopher Søren Kierkegaard, who quipped that living life with Hegel's philosophy was like trying to find your way around Copenhagen with a map of Europe. He considered Hegel's thinking ill-equipped to aid in the daily struggle of becoming an individual. Kierkegaard vehemently believed that Hegel had forgotten something essential: *existence*. Kierkegaard formalized existence as a category of philosophical thinking and thus gave birth to existentialism. For the existentialists, humans do not exist in the same way that other things do, but are rather defined by their choices and their possibilities. In other words, humans have *to decide and act* in order to exist beyond their Aristotelian definition of "featherless bipeds." This requires more than simply the decision to wear a black turtleneck and beret while smoking Gauloises on the Left Bank. One has to define oneself in a particular way—one has to become what one is. *Ecce Homo.*

3.

The interplay of being and becoming in eternity and history seem to be the *OH, my GOD!! Yes!!* but why I am thinking about this *now, YESSS!!* while being *AH!* spanked by a German *Führer* in a Copenhagen bathhouse? Sweet Jesus, darling, something *is* rotten in Denmark but it feels so *fresh.* Why was I *mein Gott!* thinking about all this? Was it Kierkegaard in Copenhagen? Or the mustached German, whose firm and manly spanking had the bite and sting of so many mordant Nietzschean aphorisms? Perhaps it was the bathhouse itself, dark and dank, reminiscent of the diseased respite offered by an old asylum. It was a hospital filled with corridors, dimly lit rooms with doors invitingly ajar, offering instant therapies in the thick and salubrious atmosphere of steam and smoke. *Nietzsche went insane.* A labyrinth of sin, a dusky den of iniquity—but a psychiatry ward? Or perhaps a maternity ward where fathers and sons covered in towels and sweat circle aimlessly while women are off giving birth to something real. *"Wah! WAAAAAH!"* I wanted to cry out, but no matter how hard my bare bottom was being slapped, I could not capture a true breath. One must first be able to capture a true breath before crying out.

My head began to swell. A helium balloon, it rose high and hovered, buoyant on the turbulent streams of steam above. I was held in tow by a mysterious string and walked through the circus grounds, my head bouncing around with the rollicking view from above. I saw the ant farm of male sexuality in its full mindless force. More laughable than erotic, eyes met for a shade more than an instant and then—for reasons unknown—men coupled, decoupled, and recoupled. I was again being tugged from down under as my gaseous intellect precipitated out of the steam and was reattached to my rubbery flesh below. I was getting spanked by daddy and *I could not breathe.*

The son rose and suddenly felt a power over all of them. Inspired by hash and sex, I stood erect and danced naked as their withered eyes became transfixed with longing by my vermicular writhing. I caressed my abdomen, smooth and brown, taut and rippled. *Ecce Homo.* They stared with the forlorn knowledge that they had them once, long before they became tarred and feathered with fat and hair.

I was getting sucked, in a theater, a Cartesian theater of the absurd. A circus, a post-modern cabaret, movie flickering with soundless clips disjointed of flesh and old girlfriends, high school English teacher, lights and torrid affairs, the hash hitting me, *getting sucked*, more flickering clips from the cutting-room floor of a discarded past, remembering future fantasy, gliding down the frictionless slide of a nameless event horizon, swirling down a vortex, swirling wordlessly, swirling silently down an endless black drain of *orgasm*.

4.

Men or women—when it came to sex I saw little difference at the time. I regarded the modernist view with contempt: clinging to the illusion of stable sexual structures and objects, "homo-" and "hetero-" sexuality were treated as erotic realities rather than reified conventions. Given the vast choices of animal, vegetable, or mineral, I felt righteous in my orthodoxy if I was trafficking within the narrow confines of *Homo sapiens*. Even a prude like Nietzsche tells us coquettishly that "the degree *and kind* of a man's sexuality reach up into the ultimate pinnacle of his experience."[1] We cannot escape the fact that *animus* and *anima* are in constant struggle and constant flux: one can never step into the same sexuality twice.

After all, a penis is a much closer relative to a clitoris than it is to a nuclear warhead or a stalagmite. A pitted avocado chopped in half has more family resemblance to a banana than it does to the body of a mandolin. The freakiness begins when you start breeding avocados and stalagmites, or something of this sort: transsexuality is endocrinology gone absolutely mad. Smooth and hairless remnants of atrophied testicles get tucked and nestled in a silicone-packed ass, while Plasticine tits are prominently displayed on a mantle of pectoralis that simply will not shrink from the challenge of the new identity. "I sucka yo deek?" an Asian tart grins and queeries, the lumps in her panties almost as large as the ones in her bra, *"I sucka yo deek?"* No, you no sucka my deek—at least not until I've snorted this last line of meth. The scene was, by all who participated, an intense longing for womanhood and the players themselves were not so much feminine as grotesque caricatures thereof. It was the natural longing rather than the natural possession of femininity that characterized these transsexuals. They tried to capture elusive mysteries with grossly exaggerated posturing and overdone trappings—and that was precisely the sad point of it all. What women tease out with nuance, men strike with a hammer.

5.

Why had I been thinking of Nietzsche? Was it the German? The mustache? The futile attempt of sexually becoming what one is? No, the moment now comes to me: *it was the eternal recurrence, the question of time that recollected me.* For in several hours I would board the train to Elsinore (*Seams, madam? I know not seams*) and lecture on the nature of time. This required an efficient change from moist towel to crisp suit and tie, and so I made haste to my hostel in Copenhagen, pausing only to contemplate on the grave of Kierkegaard.

The train ride to Elsinore cut a swath through a northern

dawn that cast an ever more beautiful light on the straits separating Denmark from Sweden. I heard many lecturers on the train introducing themselves and chattering about this theory and that. There were many ghosts in the field, who seemed to clutch at the mists and vapors of other ghosts. I wondered if they had ever considered Nietzsche's view that

> Philosophy, as I have so far understood it, means living voluntarily among ice and high mountains—seeking out everything strange and questionable in existence, everything so far placed under a ban by morality.[2]

Philosophy: a seeking-out, not simply a talking-about. So many ghosts, so many shades around me, but I was still taut with excitement. I was anxious to meet the few passionate ones who would live for it—or better yet, who would *die* for it. It would be the first time in my young graduate-school career that I would rise and speak to the community of thinkers. It would be the first time I would bare myself and say: *Ecce Homo.*

philosophy and a young maiden

1.

Philosophy was not simply in my brain but in my blood. My parents each had come from a prominent philosophical lineage, a bloodline to which I would become an unworthy heir. They were introduced in Cambridge during their doctoral studies at Harvard: Karl had recently moved from Germany and met my mother Helen at a party hosted by other Europeans in the area. She had also moved from the Continent, her father having transplanted the family from Greece for an endowed professorship. Between their interest and involvement in the world of philosophy and their origin in the world of Europe, they shared a common ground that fostered an immediate affinity. Both families were effusive when the young couple announced their wedding plans and the hope for a grandchild was expectorated in virtually the same breath. The grandmothers were anxious for a little one and the grandfathers beamed with pride at the thought of their two noble philosophical traditions made flesh. When I was born, I was received like the bizarre lovechild of Plato and Hegel.

However, as my grandmother poignantly described to me, these early years were not a happy time for my parents. Displaced from Europe, challenged in their graduate studies, and under financial duress, they felt the fault lines of immaturity start to gape and rupture. Stress driving them to alcohol, drugs, and other lovers, this beautiful couple soon turned ugly. First they lost their center, then they lost their love, and finally they lost their minds. Karl left Harvard and the apartment in Cambridge. My mother was broken, and then she, too, went away.

At five years of age I was taken to Amherst to live with my grandparents. It was then that I embarked upon my first philosophical investigation: an inquiry into the nature of attachment and separation.

"Why do we love someone and why do we miss them when they go away?"

Such stories from my youth, which I never even remembered in order to forget, are somehow shocking. So often one recalls the events of adolescence as the beginning of an adult history, the hormones of pubescence flowing like a Lethe that makes us forget the self that was always there in some strange way.

At the age of seven, I was sent to a child psychologist after writing a school story about the mutilation of my father by mountain lions. The pretty doctor would sit on the floor with me and watch me draw pictures or play games. I would tell her about my dreams of living in the aquarium and she would listen intently and smile. Months later, for the same class, I submitted a story about marrying my doctor and drew a picture of us lying in bed together. I will never forget the teacher's response, which was delivered much like an oracle.

"Dorian, you have a very brilliant side ... but you also have a very *evil* side."

I cried myself to sleep that night, not knowing that I could have rested my weary head on an aphorism such as "there are no moral phenomena at all, but only a moral interpretation of phenomena."[3] Oh, Nietzsche—why *are* you so clever?

2.

Some twenty-five years before he wrote *Ecce Homo*, a teenage Friedrich started another form of memoir, entitled *Euphorion*. The work was to be a novel about a world-weary man searching out his *Doppelgänger* so that the evil twin might dissect his brain. The fragments that remain suggest themes of incest, murder, and other "strange and questionable" subjects of philosophy that the young Nietzsche was exploring. The evil *Doppelgänger*, or double, is the fantasy of many a serious mind and to bring it into being is the task of a serious will. I wonder if this is what Pascal meant when he noted that anyone can go to an extreme—but only the great can touch both extremes at once.

3.

Throughout adolescence my intellectual prowess shone brighter and my early essays on the history of philosophy signaled a developing acumen. I successfully applied to the most cerebral college I could find, where I would study philosophy with other highly disturbed individuals. Sensitive minds are most susceptible to injury, and, in the spirit of Wilhelm Reich, can develop the hardest armor for their defense. This is why the mark of the academic is never simply intelligence, but *critical* intelligence. Fortunately, undergraduate philosophy still has the naive but inspiring rituals of late-night metaphysics over reefer, wine, and cigarettes. Like, what does it all *mean*, man?

My senior thesis on Hegel was well received, and although an inconsistent student, I was nonetheless encouraged to continue my studies on the graduate level. Burned out by the scene, I avoided this path, spending time after college simply reading and thinking. While pleasurable on its surfaces, it became clear that the contemplative life can easily slide down the slippery slope to the vegetative life—dissatisfaction and shame began to rear their ugly heads. Suddenly, each book I read became a judgment, each essay a condemnation of my own laziness and inadequacy. The great philosophers became overachieving big brothers to whom I was constantly being compared. Day after day I would endure a nagging bitch of a superego berating me. "*Nietzsche* was a professor of philology at Basel when he was only *twenty-four, before* his doctorate was even *conferred. You* can't even get your shit together to *apply* to graduate school at the age of *twenty-five.*" Or "*Wittgenstein* fought on the front lines of World War I while writing the *Tractatus Logico-Philosophicus*, a work that secured his place in the pantheon of philosophical geniuses. *You* can't even scratch your ass and twiddle your balls at the same time without getting confused." Unable to withstand the ponderous burden of being rather than doing, I assembled an application for graduate school.

This all begs the question of why I embarked upon the graduate study of philosophy in the first place. Was it a desire for the field, or merely a desire to structure and occupy my thoughts? Was

I avoiding the search for my own calling by simply adopting the calling of my family? Was I overflowing with a love for philosophy, or was philosophy filling the lack of love? The truth is, I never really knew why I was doing what I was doing—do any of us? Freud said that sometimes a cigar is just a cigar. If only it were that simple. The problem is that the cigar is always a cigar *and* always a penis—so you never quite know why you're putting it in your mouth.

4.

I finally submitted an application, and I was invited to interview at the University. Responding to my interest in studying Nietzsche, my first interview was scheduled with the famous Dr. Hans Regelstein. Having written a comprehensive treatise of Nietzsche's thought that was considered by some to rival those of Jaspers and Heidegger, Regelstein had made a name for himself within the academy. Bald on top with a cherubic halo of gold and orange locks, old Hans sported an impressive mustache much like Nietzsche's own. He was a tall, broad-shouldered German, with a chiseled jaw that framed a beguiling smile. His physical presence had the dimensions of a laborer rather than a philosopher, and indeed his own father was a blacksmith. Regelstein, too, liked to hammer out ideas—but no longer seemed to strike while the iron was hot. Once an impressive thinker, he had become an even more impressive politician. Iced over with a cordial American veneer that would cloy any discerning palate, he was nonetheless a German "Herr Doktor Professor" at the core. It would take me years to learn that his seemingly casual behavior concealed a desire to have the lips of his students loyally affixed to his ass, while lips that instead expressed original ideas were punished with the passive-aggressive kiss of death.

Most old and bitter couples once had sweet, romantic beginnings, and so it goes with mentors and students. Although it is difficult to imagine that such a mind once needed guidance, Nietzsche also had a series of mentors. His first was Arthur Schopenhauer, the notoriously cantankerous German who was a contemporary of Hegel. While Hegel asserted the Idea as fundamental to the world, Schopenhauer's *Meisterwerk* asserted *Will* as the fundamental force of the universe. His profound pessimism directed us to the inherent misery of our existence, ever subject to the striving of Will. It was the consideration of this suffering that led Schopenhauer to the exploration of Hindu and Buddhist thought, and it was he who introduced this influence to the Western canon. Schopenhauer offered us only temporary relief from our wretchedness, primarily through the aesthetic and the ascetic paths of existence. Schopenhauer, in essence, responded to life with a resounding *No*.

When Nietzsche first encountered Schopenhauer's work, it was an epiphany. He was early on in his studies of philology at Leipzig and *The World as Will and Representation* stimulated an intense interest in philosophy. Schopenhauer filled the void that his renunciation of Christianity and theology had left and inspired him to a new level of seriousness and self-exploration. In the end, however, Nietzsche repudiated Schopenhauer's pessimism. God was dead, and the stakes were high for a Europe teetering on the precipice of nihilism. While Schopenhauer said *No*, Nietzsche wanted to teach the world to say *Yes*.

This was the context in which Nietzsche would ultimately formulate the concept of the eternal recurrence of the moment. With the death of God, the untenability of metaphysics, the limitations of science, and the irrational basis of the world, mankind was in a position to turn its eyes away in despair. While Hegel tried to show that each moment was the culmination of all previous moments as the dialectic unfolded to the future goal of Freedom, Nietzsche was postulating that each moment would come back to us *unchanged* and for an *eternity*. But how did this solve the problem of nihilism? Isn't it more encouraging to have the hope of future progress rather than being condemned to each moment lived over and over and over again unchanged?

5.

My final interview was scheduled with Dr. Arielle Tempe, the chair of the Philosophy Department at the University. Dr. Tempe was a behemoth of a woman, with a rat's nest of kinky black wire on her head, and breath that could wither the cedars of Lebanon. She nonetheless flew in the philosophical stratosphere and the eager student could therefore not help but be attracted to her. Speaking with electrifying erudition about Nietzsche and his contemporaries, she wove an intricate tapestry out of the threads of art, literature, and philosophy. She seemed genuinely excited when I expressed a desire to make him the focus of my dissertation. Rising, arm outstretched, she offered her hand and an acceptance to the program. Enthralled by her eloquence, as well as the chance to work with Regelstein, I agreed to come. Our grasp lingering for a hint beyond the appropriate, I became aroused and nervous. She suggested we celebrate over a beer and I smiled in acquiescence, a starstruck schoolgirl.

As I walked beside her toward the local University pub, I felt the warmth of an adolescent crush washing over me. We entered the dark and smoky cellar, but puppy love transformed the whole scene for me. I was suddenly bathing in bright lights and big-band music, as the beer-drenched bar became clean white linoleum, my pint of ale a malted shake, and my cigarette the accompanying straw. I was back in an age in which I never lived, my knees nervously knocking below my skirt and above my bobby socks. Dr. Tempe was the high-school quarterback who I hoped would soon pin me and ask me to the prom. My head tilted coyly, my big dark eyes ablaze with the innocent thrill of Christmas morn, I listened enraptured to tall tales about the philosophical touchdowns of days gone by. "Did you really inspire Gadamer to take a new direction of hermeneutic thinking? Did you *really* stump Quine on a central point of Frege's *Begriffsschrift*?" Mmmmmmmmm . . . *dreamy*.

Suddenly, however, we were back in the bar. Her persona abruptly deflating, Dr. Tempe turned from her past glory to her present misery. Her husband, she confided with a drunken stage whisper, had become increasingly withdrawn over the past decade, developing more of a taste for booze than for her. *Why is it that men so often seem to disappear and where is it, exactly, that they go?* Becoming distraught with a lability that only ethanol can fuel, she admitted that she and her husband had not had sex "for *years*." Head down, nodding in dismay, she reached for my hand on the bar. Leaning into me, she became the girl again and I brought her to my chest to soothe her. She turned up tenuously to offer her mouth, a newborn bird wanting food from mommy. My instinct to make love to her was matched only by my instinct to destroy her—which end of the cigar would I suck upon?

In my hotel room we undressed quickly, hands rapidly alternating between our clothes and each other. We kissed and suckled with a passion so intense that it could have little to do with either of us in that moment in time. Her skin was dry and my fingers appreciated the rough surface that recorded a history of shedding and molting. She was corpulent and misshapen, with a moist red warmth lurking behind her pendulous breasts and burgeoning belly. She sat on the edge of the bed, peering up seductively, her head cocked and lips pursed. I stood naked and erect in front of her, finding her comically ugly until, quite suddenly and to my surprise, she transformed. I discerned the lithe shape of youth fluidly undulating deep within her: she was still *woman*, and as such, was infinitely more beautiful than the most beautiful man. Arms outstretched behind her, hands planted on the bed, her head fell slowly back as she opened her legs, a sacred offering of burnt ashes.

Who was she in that moment? Who was I to her? Many questions were spinning in my drunken head, but as Epictetus once said, there is little competition between philosophy and a young maiden. I suppose the same is true for an old one as well.

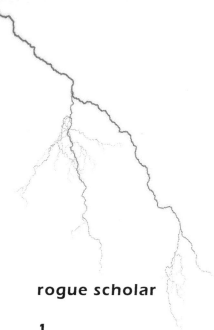

rogue scholar

1.

I was a womanizer in graduate school. A notorious womanizer. A highly talented and unequivocally nefarious womanizer. Throughout my illustrious career of womanizing, however, I never bothered to investigate what the word actually *meant*. This is not, admittedly, what one would call a fundamental philosophical project, but it is quite important nonetheless. First, it should be stated that *womanizer* is emphatically not synonymous with *lady's man*. A lady's man should be considered in contradistinction to a *man's man*, namely, an individual of the male sex who abides by an ethos that is in accord with that of his fellow men, rather than that of other women. Clearly, by definition, and by Aristotle's law of non-contradiction, a lady's man cannot be a man's man—but a womanizer most certainly can. A lady's man, as opposed to a man's man, might sleep with his best friend's wife, but this does not of necessity fall under the auspices of womanizing. No, womanizing seems to be a distinct endeavor.

The word itself is quite curious. *Womanizer* is a noun and *womanize* a verb, both having their stem and root in *woman*. But this *ize* seems a strange addition, no? Proselytize, synthesize, and mesmerize are all rather different than womanize, for the *ize* seems to be somehow inherent. Proselytize is to preach in order to convert, synthesize to bring together, and mesmerize to evoke a state of trance. The term *womanize*, however, seems to have more family resemblance to a word like *legitimize*. To legitimize is to *make legitimate*, thus, the *ize* of this type of verb implies a kind of "making" of whatever the root is. We can postulate, therefore, that to *womanize* means to *make woman* and that a *womanizer* is *one who makes woman*. A *womanizer* now sounds more like a tool or instrument of sorts, something along the lines of a *tenderizer*. A tenderizer is a little steel hammer, with multiple protrusions on the facets of its cuboid surface that vaguely resemble the pleasure bumps on condoms available in the bathrooms of European discotheques. The process of tenderizing is quite simple. One takes the hammer firmly in hand, repeatedly beats on the recalcitrant piece of meat, and—*voila!*—one *makes tender*. But how does a womanizer *make woman*? What is the little steel hammer and what the recalcitrant piece of meat? Is there some form of proto-woman from which woman is made? Is the process of making woman something like the process of becoming what one is? Indeed, a treatise of this subject would be a mighty and valuable tome.

There are, however, a few crucial points that can be noted. A womanizer should never mythologize—that is within the domain of the lady's man. The lady's man has as his cheap trade the romantic objectification of woman and he will invariably be despised for it. Next, when one wishes to womanize, one should never infantilize. In order to *make woman*, one must be a man, not a daddy. The paternalistic impulse to treat a female like a frail and innocent girl may earn the admiration of a wayward waif, but women worth their salt will find it intolerable. Conversely, a womanizer should not gratuitously sexualize. Sexuality certainly has its place in womanizing, but one should avoid the inclination to *make whore* as resolutely as the inclination to *make angel* or *make daughter*. Finally, those who womanize should rarely apologize. Apologies, which should be heartfelt when proffered, will have more efficacy if one employs them sparsely. They will leave the recipient with the confused emotions of appreciation, satisfaction, and a tender embarrassment for you.

There are at least two types of women for whom womanizing is inappropriate: the tough and the strong. Tough women are beyond womanizing, just as tough meat is beyond tenderizing. These women have already been womanized and in fact their spirits have often been pulverized by the evils of men, all of which has naturally led to a galvanized state that will defend against the best, as well as the worst, intentions. The strong woman is yet another entity. Her femininity will not be energized by womanizing, as she does not need a man to organize or catalyze the necessary reactions to *make woman*. It is best to steer clear of the tough and the strong, if successful womanizing is the goal. One should be content, in the alternative, to drink whiskey and smoke cigarettes with the former, and marry the latter.

2.

Although I had long admired her, I did not actually meet Phaedre until my second year of graduate school. By sheer chance, we sat down next to each other at the annual Al-dada lecture. Al-dadaism was an intellectual force at the university and its main proponent was as charismatic as he was strange. A former Muslim philosopher in Baghdad, Professor Al-dada was reputed to have ingested some ergot-contaminated bread on a pilgrimage to Mecca. The ensuing trip from this natural psychedelic evoked visions of a seamless synthesis of Islamic mysticism and Martin Heidegger's philosophy. The bizarre but profound work that was spawned was a Sufi allegory embodying Heidegger's fundamental ontology. Each year, Al-dada would speak with enthralling brilliance and his controversial ideas left no doubt as to why he received a harsh *fatwa* in the Muslim world. Phaedre and I seemed to be easing closer and closer during his discussion of Sufi sexual enlightenment, and before the applause died down we began to speak.

"Good to finally meet you, Dorian, I'm Phaedre."

"Does your name come from the play of Racine?"

"Yes, precisely!"

"I translated the work from French as an undergraduate and once published an essay comparing it to the original *Hippolytus*."

"*Really*. That is quite interesting. I would love to hear your thoughts about it sometime."

"Why don't we grab a drink tomorrow night and chat?"

She blushed. "I would enjoy that. *Hippolytus* was written by Sophocles, yes?"

"Yes, if my memory serves me!"

I too was flush with excitement and the fact that I already had both a delightful girlfriend and a trashy mistress did not in the least dampen my desire to unlock the mysteries awaiting me behind those inscrutable gray eyes and beneath that rich crimson hair. My memory did, in fact, serve me. I knew, of course, that *Hippolytus* was written by Euripides rather than Sophocles, but I dared not correct, for fear of endangering the coming play of Testicles— the author of all of my tragedy.

3.

Nietzsche divided Greek civilization into two opposing forces: the Apollonian and the Dionysian. Apollo was the God of Light and Dionysus the God of Intoxication. The Apollonian elements of culture were those of order, rationality, and individuality, and were most clearly manifested in the art of sculpture. The Dionysian forces, on the other hand, were states that subjugated the individual to a greater whole, such as intoxication, sex, and ecstasies. He considered the purest form of Dionysian art to be music, which is capable of accessing reality unhindered by the constraints of representation. Nietzsche argued that the tension of these forces is necessary for Greek tragedy, an argument he proffered in his first work, *The Birth of Tragedy*. The book was published several years after his appointment at Basel, to the praise of his friend and mentor Richard Wagner and to the condemnation of his philological colleagues. Nietzsche would always embrace the Dionysian aspects in his philosophy and thus he broke with the tradition of the philosopher as an advocate of reason and order. His love of the Dionysian is curious given his passionate commitment to the self-creation of the individual, a seemingly Apollonian endeavor—or does one need to lose oneself in order to become what one is?

It is somehow hard to imagine the frail and sensitive Nietzsche in an ecstatic frenzy with the Bacchae, the worshipers of Dionysus who were depicted by Euripides. The Bacchae, or Maenads (literally, the "raving ones"), indulged in drunkenness, violence, bloodletting, self-mutilation, and sex with reckless abandon, and were considered by Greek society to be beyond the reach of reason. King Pentheus of Thebes condemned the Bacchae because they did not recognize his divinity, and he paid dearly for it. After being lured into the woods, Pentheus was decapitated and his corpse further mutilated by Agave—his own mother. This haunting image from Euripides recalls an aphorism from Nietzsche: "In revenge and in love woman is more barbarous than man."[4]

4.

I paid homage to Apollo and Dionysus in equal measure. Strangely, however, the rational Apollonian order of my days was spent in reflection on a philosopher who extolled the Dionysian, while the Dionysian frenzy of my nights was structured by a cryptic Apollonian order that would take me long to discover.

A day in the life. A good Friday. A portrait of the philosopher as a young asshole. In the first event of the day, I delivered a colloquium on Immanuel Kant and the nature of time, in preparation for an upcoming talk in Denmark. In the Transcendental Aesthetic of his *Critique of Pure Reason*, Kant put forth the argument that space and time are not physical realities, but rather functions of the mind. In other words, space and time are not objective entities perceived *by* consciousness, but rather modes *of* consciousness that help put form to a formless world. This view is not consistent with classical physics, which posits an absolute space and time existing independently of the mind of man. After the theory of relativity, however, the notion of absolute time was no longer tenable. This is due to the fact that given events "A" and "B," it can be said with equal validity (depending on the frame of reference of the observer) that "A" happened at the same time as "B," before "B," or after "B." Based on this, the Austrian logician and mathematician Kurt Gödel (a neurotic genius famous for his incompleteness theorems) argued against the reality of time, claiming that relativity theory supports Kantian philosophy. It is a testimony to the introspective genius of Kant that he could, in the eighteenth century, foresee a twentieth-century notion of time. Although time is given to our minds *a priori* according to Kant, could it not also be a substrate on which further experience acts? If there is no objective time and time is a mode of consciousness, then could it not be modulated on the basis of conscious experience?

The discussion rolls on an hour past the allotted time and spills into the coffeehouse afterward. I am feeling energized and particularly charged to see Phaedre in the audience, especially as we begin to discuss the nature of time, standing very close to one another in space, gratuitously touching each other on the shoulder or the hand, every veiled caress filling me with warmth, but then we part, effusing about the night to come, which seemingly takes forever to arrive, but then does and takes off with red wine and tender filet and an endless chain of cigarettes and conversation about my interests in Nietzsche and her interests in Foucault, all feeding into the connection of French politics and French philosophy and—French wine?, more Bordeaux?, I would love some, yes, thank you and, oh excuse me Phaedre, I didn't mean to, but the bump spontaneously coalesces into an embrace and the spilled wine is massaged into her breasts as the fetters of Apollo fall fast to form a soft floor for our Dionysian ecstasies, and in the glow of firelight crimson hair flows out like blood, which would soon trickle—then pour—from the nails in my back and the teeth in my shoulders, the pain flipping the switch to some deep electric current of fear and force that animates every muscle, force flirting with violence as I repay in kind with hand on throat, received with moans and nodding head and gasp for air, as we are pushed beyond the precipice, down the abyss, into the catacombs, and through the labyrinths . . . never truly to return.

We parted tenderly, Phaedre seeing me to the door wrapped in a hot, white sheet spotted with my blood. We kissed and she wished me pleasant dreams. Although we had said our goodbyes and goodnights, I wasn't even close to calling it a day. It was never enough to serve only Apollo and Dionysus—I needed to worship the false and jealous God of *More*. *More* alcohol, *more* sex, *more* experience, *more* worship celebrating hunger rather than life. Those with a bottomless belly need a city, a place where the trough is always open to feed. If you want it, there it is, waiting for you, late at night, the time and the place where a double life can transform into a triple life, all with very little effort, because everyone out at that hour is hungry for something: alcohol, money, drugs, sex. Alcohol and drugs feed the hunger for sex, which money can buy. Selling your sex brings in money, which can be used for drugs or alcohol. Drugs can be sold or bartered to get sex or other drugs. The more money you are willing to give up, the more sex you can get; the more sex you are willing to give up, the more money you can get. The more money you have, the more drugs you can get. The more drugs you can get, the more sex you can have. Alcohol, money, drugs, and sex: products that do not require a customer rewards program, because everyone will be back, because everyone needs *more*. *More*, I love you! *More*, I need you more than love! *More*, I worship you! *More*, I fall on my knees and suck for you! *More*, only you can truly fill the void! *More*, I turn my life over to you! *More*, you reign in the kingdom of pimps and whores! *More*, you are the patron saint of pushers and users! *More*, I shall have no other God! *More*, whose essence is *never enough*! *More*, whose name is *the Mind*! Impassioned, I suddenly and quite unexpectedly find myself ripping-off Ginsberg—and doing a shitty job of it, at that.

She looked normal enough, but a young woman standing on the dark corner of abandoned city streets at 4:00 a.m. looking "normal enough" should have immediately filled me with mistrust of either her or myself. As I approached, I sensed something stirring. I wondered what she wanted, what she needed, and what she was willing to give in return. How did I know she wanted or needed anything? *Her eyes told me.* They were not weary eyes that passed over mine for a random moment on the way to closing after being nestled in a warm pillow in a warm home. No, these were glassy urgent eyes that were fixed upon mine, desperate trapped-animal eyes that told me: *I have needs. I have needs that make me disavow my past and disregard my future. I have needs that bring me to you in the here and the now. I have needs—and nothing else matters, moth-erfucker.* In the midst of all the chaos and the dirt, there was such a clean and elegant simplicity to it all. Kierkegaard wrote a book entitled *Purity of Heart Is to Will One Thing.* If this is true, then I can only begin to imagine the snow-white heart of this dark angel who willed nothing but *crack cocaine.*

Here was the deal: she wanted it, badly, and knew where to get it. My gig was to pay for the cab, pay "the man" for "the rock," and then we could both go back to her place to "get lit," and she would treat me "real good," and she was "real happy" not to smoke with "them moolies and spics."

"So, you wanna smoke crack with me?"

It was an interesting question. Just hours earlier someone had asked me if I could reconcile Kant's transcendental epistemology with non-Euclidean geometry. The phrase "smoke crack," however, somehow rattled me. Perhaps if she had offered the inhalation of a central nervous system stimulant produced by a reaction in which the acid "cocaine hydrochloride" is conjugated with a base under warm aqueous conditions in order to form a paste that is ultimately desiccated to a solidified and combustible substance, I might have felt more comfortable. The phrase "smoke crack," however, conjured up the image of desperate HIV-laden junkies, fellating coke whores, inexorable addiction, ruined lives. I recognized that I was crossing a dangerous line, I thought about it carefully . . . and then I greedily said *Yes.*

The acquisition of the . . . combustible stimulant . . . was rela-tively unremarkable. I merely provided the capital and waited pa-tiently in the cab for the dividends to return, hoping only that my philosophy books would be divided among friends after I was murdered. It was then a short and relatively inexpensive cab ride from the war zone where we purchased to the post-apocalyptic wasteland where we would ultimately consume. Her apartment was decorated in a style somewhere between minimalist and Spartan, which made sense considering that the only room she wished to furnish fully was the one in her coke-hungry brain.

The consumption apparatus itself was quite comical. For someone who was a career junkie, I would have expected paraphernalia of a more durable quality. Instead, I was handed an empty plastic soda bottle with a small aperture cut for inhalation, and a tin foil cradle on the open top where the small white rock was placed. I spread my lips on the hole and deeply inhaled as she lit the solidified $C_{17}H_{21}NO_4$ mixed with ash and *whoooooooooooooooooooooooooosh*, the cool rape of the lungs followed by a soft fallback with closed eyes to witness the time-lapse stardust shower from a supernova of euphoria and warmth and *Ye-e-ess, everything in life is O. . . . . . K. . . . . . .*

Minutes later, I was both coming down and tweaking up. She continued to smoke with the concentration of a surgeon, but then suddenly went down on all fours, angry, sniffing around like a dog, scouring the thick shag carpet for any morsel of cocaine she could scavenge. She needed *More*, she said—she needed to make another run. Her eyes became wild, staring at me with rage and desperation. She demanded another twenty dollars and a promise that I would be there when she returned. I gave her both. Promise me you'll be here when I get back. I promise. Promise me you'll be here when I get back. I promise. Promise me you'll be here when I get back. I promise. Terrified, I left the moment I could.

What made the experience so disturbing was not so much the feeling that she "wasn't there" because of her addiction, but rather the feeling that I wasn't there. I was looked through and talked at. I was not living anywhere near that Kantian moral Utopia where everyone is an end in themselves, but rather a stark world in which I was nothing more than a vector, a means to an end, a vehicle that would deliver her to the destination of crack and thereafter be useless. As I nervously shuffled through empty streets, hopped-up and hailing cabs that were passing only in my hallucinations, I thought of my behavior earlier in the night. Was Phaedre simply a vector? Were all of the women mere vehicles? Were they treated as ends in themselves, or only means to satisfy the hunger of my mind? It was too much to think about, too complicated to consider at the time. All I knew was that Phaedre and I had developed a special bond that night, a bond much deeper than love. It was that special, sentimental bond between lovers who have mutually revealed the instinct to kill and the desire to die.

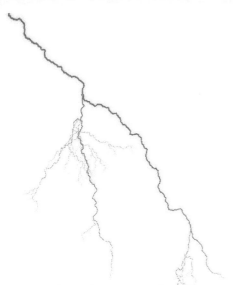

the dream of the corals

1.

John Maynard Keynes wrote a book on the economic implications of the Treaty of Versailles that predicted the peril of post-war Germany while Hitler was still busy flunking out of art school in Austria. *The General Theory of Employment, Interest, and Money* ushered in the new era of macroeconomics and his philosophical treatise on probability stands as a classic. The real brilliance of Keynes, however, was that he could still take pleasure in donning a pink dress and prancing around a party with his fellow "Apostles," the semi-secret members of a gay society at the University of Cambridge.

It has been suggested that the depressed and alcoholic Hegel had an on-going incestuous affair with his sister. Socrates was reputed by some to have engaged in bigamy, marrying Myrto while already wed to Xanthippe. Diogenes the Cynic would masturbate in public, wryly noting that he wished he could also relieve his hunger by simply stroking his belly. Foucault reached the pinnacle of the intellectual elite with his appointment to the Collège de France, but still knew how to slap leather to ass in an S&M club when the spirit moved him. Nietzsche himself was once thought to have gone mad from the neurologic sequelae of syphilis, contracted in a bordello during his adolescence. In the end, it seems that every true and healthy intellect discovers that there is nothing quite so philosophically stimulating as highbrow debauchery.

2.

I had completed the required courses for my PhD and passed the comprehensive examination that enabled me to enter the category of ABD—All But Dissertation. I would now have to engage in an intensive study of Nietzsche's work in order to unravel his reasoning behind the eternal return, as well as extensive research of the secondary literature on the subject. I knew I could never accomplish this at the university, as it had become a far too constraining environment. I had become all but estranged from my advisor Regelstein because of his insistence that I follow his line of inquiry rather than my own. What was the purpose of my doctoral work, if not to become a critical and independent thinker? How could he be an expert, when he was precisely the kind of philosopher that Nietzsche himself would despise?

In my romantic life, I was walking on pins and needles, supported by a fragile bed of eggshells, laid carefully atop a minefield resting on thin ice. I had earned a peculiar notoriety through my lusty escapades, and the trail of bitterness and betrayal was immeasurably long and impressively complicated. In my first year of graduate school I had a reputation for being duplicitous, but by the end of the third I had progressed to "triplicitous," and had even once been angrily—and quite unjustly—accused of "quadruplicity." Fortunately, my diligence in the first years of graduate school served me well, and I was granted asylum via the Dimlit Scholarship for International Study. The University was pleased and proud of this accomplishment, but no one was more pleased to leave than I. I knew there was only one place I wanted to go and when I actually arrived in Berlin, I passed through customs paying homage to Oscar Wilde: "I have nothing to declare . . . except my genius."

3.

There are several reasons why Berlin has such a heaviness, and one is quite clearly the weather. For most of the year the sun makes a feeble appearance behind thick clouds at 8:00 a.m. and retreats from the relentless rains at 3:30 or 4:00 in the afternoon. It is difficult to be blithe in the midst of such gloom, but there are far deeper reasons. As a massive body can bend space around it, so do cataclysmic events and individuals seem to restructure the very fabric of a city. Berlin was the focus of the world in the first half of the twentieth century and the focus of *two* worlds in the second. Hitler, the Nazis, and the Berlin Wall have all left indelible imprints in our historical memory. Berlin embodies the power of German thought and German destruction. Hegel and Schopenhauer had once taught at the Humboldt University; Einstein, Marx, and Planck had all studied there. Within minutes from the Humboldt, however, exist the remains of the concentration camp Sachsenhausen. At the entrance, one sees the chilling inscription "Arbeit Macht Frei"—work sets you free. The final exit for many, however, was Station Z—the gas chamber where the first Nazi experiments in mass murder took place. One can hear three operas every night in Berlin and can also hear the cold air from the river Spree hissing to hell like the 100,000 Russians who died while capturing her. Despite this weight, or rather precisely *because* of it, Berlin has its own *Doppelgänger*: debauchery. From the 1920s onward, Berlin has been a place to get fucked up faster than Jesse Owens ran the hundred when he was there for the '36 Olympics. The clubs, cafés, and Cabarets still abound. As a result, Berlin is a city with both a hip edge and a dark *gravitas*. My scholarship was a first-class ride that delivered me to this Holy Land of death and abandon and shortly thereafter burst into flames like the fucking Hindenburg. Scholar? *Drunk*. Drug addict. Thinker. *God*.

4.

Through my research, I discovered that Nietzsche had various lines of logic for positing the eternal recurrence of the moment. The rationale, the Apollonian basis, was described in *The Will to Power*. Nietzsche put forth the argument that the world is comprised of a certain finite quantity of force, as the notion of infinite force would be self-contradictory. Because there is a definite quantity of force, then the combination of forces would have to be calculable as a finite number. Assuming that time is infinite, each finite combination of forces would have to occur repeatedly *ad infinitum* and each event would influence the overall sequence of the series. From these premises, Nietzsche concluded that the series of moments that comprise our life will by necessity be repeated *ad infinitum*, as the "great dice game" of existence plays out forever.

Theoretical physics has arguments both for and against this line of reasoning. However, the concept of eternal recurrence is essentially metaphysical and there was also an existential logic behind it. Nietzsche introduces this in *The Gay Science* and further expands the idea in *Thus Spoke Zarathustra*. In *The Gay Science*, Nietzsche asks us to imagine the following:

> What, if some day or night a demon were to steal after you into your loneliest loneliness and say to you: "This life as you now live it and have lived it, you will have to live once more and innumerable times more, and there will be nothing new in it, but every pain and every joy and every thought and sigh and everything unutterably small or great in your life will have to return to you, all in the same succession and sequence—even this spider and this moonlight between the trees, and even this moment and I myself. The eternal hourglass of existence is turned upside down again and again, and you with it, speck of dust!"[5]

He then goes on to inquire about the consequences of this. Understandably, your response to the demon will depend on the moment in which you find yourself. If you are in your loneliest loneliness, you will "throw yourself down and gnash your teeth," but if you are experiencing a "tremendous moment," then you will praise the demon as a god. Perhaps this is the Dionysian approach to the moment—when in a state of ecstasy or intoxication, one will always say *Yes* to eternal recurrence.

5.

What struck me in the first weeks of my relaxed schedule in Berlin was the burden of time. No longer on a round-the-clock crash course of things to *do*, I was forced quite simply to *be*. Each moment that should have been free and high was, in fact, quite ponderous. Without the relentless activity that was driving me in graduate school, the structure of my time was an empty stomach growling to be filled up. But why? Why this unease, this angst about an "unfilled" moment? Free from the work I had put into *becoming*, why wasn't it enough to enjoy the experience of simply *being*? Something was wrong, something out of control. The feeling of anxiety with living each day began to overtake me and the frenzied pace of my thought began to replace what was once the frenzied pace of my work. From the moment my eyes opened in the morning, until the minute they closed for an uneasy sleep, my mind was chaos, a zoo overrun with what the Zen masters called "the drunken monkeys."

Trying desperately to relax, I cultivated the habit of red wine in the evenings. A fellow scholar also enjoyed the grape, and together we would comb the charming markets in the city squares to buy cheese, bread, and a good Bordeaux. This became a ritual of sorts: sitting down with simple foods and good wine to discuss the philosophy of science, usually Popper, Kuhn, and Feyerabend. The evening ritual, however, soon became an afternoon ritual and after my colleague's family had arrived, I began to participate without company. Germans not known for their friendliness, and Berliners less so, I started to visit each club and *Kneipe* (best translated as "local watering hole") accompanied only by my thoughts and a very, very good buzz. No longer structured by academia, no longer thrusting forward from one goal and accomplishment to the next, I started to run wild. Night after night, by foot, by train, or by bike, I would explore the roiling underbelly of the blond beast, a *living* philosopher. What started out as wine and bread became a feast I would consume regularly. The menu often changed, but the same ingredients were used to cook up a cauldron full of insanity.

Chez Dorian

Aperitif
French Bordeaux
Cannabis Sativa

L'entree
Five one-half liter Hefeweizen
One pack of Gauloises Blondes

Le plat principal
Three lines of high-grade Bolivian cocaine
Six very large and delicious Black Russians
A second pack of Gauloises Blondes

Le fromage
Sex with whomever

Le dessert
Sleeping pills
Coma

Although crash-landing in bed at 4:00 or 5:00 in the morning, the relentless onslaught of thinking would begin again at 8:00 a.m. when I would spontaneously awake with a start and make my way unshowered to the Bibliotheque or the archives. My reading would be intense for several hours, but my brain had its own agenda of thought. As the haunted days of the dark and rainy autumn coursed on, it became more and more unyielding, a jealous God that demanded a flowing stream of offerings to fuel its divine ruminations. Periodically, I would be reminded that I had a body: my kidneys started to deliver punishing kicks in the back to alert me that they had not tasted a non-alcoholic beverage for days.

When the winter arrived, my eyes had become sunken, ripeness having passed into rot. My face was drawn and sallow, even a shade jaundiced. My fingers were stained brown from tobacco and my teeth were stained yellow. Fungus covered my feet and testicles after not showering or changing clothes for days at a time. I was finally purified. My consciousness was becoming more and more decentralized, more in tune with the strange ether that seemed to be the medium connecting everything. Eventually, nothing was a random event. Each glance had a *meaning*, each encounter delivered a *message*. The world was Mind and each of my thoughts was an event that affected its structure in some palpable way. From the nervous awakening of morning to the lying down for a good night's coma, I experienced the nearly uninterrupted train of one long thought. Philosophically, I was a burning bush: on fire, but not consumed—at least not yet.

6.

The drugs were first a daily, then an hourly event. Far from expanding my consciousness, I was using them to contain it. Each substance would redirect and focus me in its own unique way, forcing multiple and parallel paths of thinking to converge upon one. My connection, my "man," was a drummer from L.A. who frequented the Berlin jazz club that was home to a number of musically-inclined American expatriates. The host of the club, who behaved as if he were the owner, was a smack addict who maintained a steady influx but ultimately ran the place into the ground because of his habit. Stephen, however, was in control and as reliable as the German trains: when he said he was going to deliver, he *fucking delivered.*

"I've got something special, something *echt gut* for you, my man."

Smoking the grass, I realized with both anticipation and horror that it had been crop-dusted with magic. Soon, indeed, I was falling into a divine reverie—tainted only by my urgent need to vomit and defecate. Nietzsche was insightful when he noted that the abdomen is what reminds man that he isn't a God. I excused myself with the particular graciousness and meticulous composure that bespeaks a mind in sheer terror. The jazz spinning on in maddening cacophony, Stephen smiled with compassion, insight, and also a hint of *schadenfreude*—the untranslatable German term that suggests the mischievous delight in the misfortune of others.

Stumbling with dignity to the bathroom, crashing through the stall door, I fell back on the toilet after molting out of my leather pants. Fortunately I was not in a Parisian cafe, where I would have been forced to squat over a hole *comme un chien*, shitting and puking, puking and shitting, for what would be hours of purgatory. Throughout the ordeal, I am not sure if the doors of my perception were cleansed, but the walls of my gastrointestinal tract most certainly were. As the waters finally settled, my mind felt filtered and distilled. Ja—*echt gut*, my man. The latticework of grout transformed from a dirty gray to an iridescent purple, dancing a smile of Arabesque calligraphy around the smooth white teeth of the tiles. The confines of the cubicle stall began to expand and dissolve, and I started sinking slowly down. I might have been sleeping and dreaming, awake and hallucinating, or in that bizarre phantasmagorical state in between. Wherever I was, it was then that I saw, for the first time since childhood, *the corals*.

Sinking down, I was the size of a small pebble dropping through the waters of an aquarium. Blacklight on my smooth brown skin produced an eerie radiance as I passed flying fish illuminated in vivid blues, blinding limes, and atomic pinks. Stripes and spots vibrated on the scales of fantastic creatures with perpetually opened eyes that revealed nothing and sweeping frowns that no ecstasy could upturn. I felt somewhat out of place without gills, but was enraptured by the fantasia of drowning without consequence. I sank slowly, occasionally turning my face to bask in the heavenly auroras shining through the green clouds of algae above. Time seemed to slow down, but I had no regrets as I fell peacefully to the corals. A spongy bed supported me, a living nexus from which erupted the fluid stalks of the corals, undulating in an elegant sinusoidal wave on the x-axis of time and the y-axis of eternity. Atop the wiggly licorice ropes were round pink plates of smooth tissue, long thin processes reaching out from all points of the circumference, each with a bulbous end dotted with a night-blue eye. I felt so safe, so joyful, so loved, and so calm in the colorful *gurgle-gurgle* and *whoosh-whoosh*. How many times had I seen this vision as a child? And would I ever be able to wake from it, now that it was a reality?

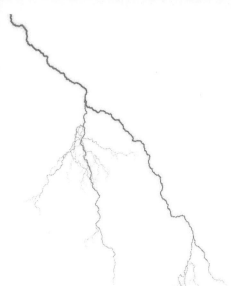

blossoming of the mindflower

1.

As the bleak winter enveloped Berlin in gloom, my thinking edged closer and closer to the precipice. One day, quite simply, it jumped off. Like the opening of a parachute during free fall, I experienced what the Buddhists call the blossoming of the mindflower. This blossoming, this *satori*, unfolded in the unlikely context of beer and Kierkegaard. Ted, a philosophy professor who was on sabbatical in Tübingen, was visiting Berlin for a Hegel conference when the core meaning of the universe was revealed to me during a philosophical bender. We were at the Café Eckstein in Prenzlauerberg at the time, a favorite venue among my academic comrades at the Humboldt. As Ted and I began philosophizing, it was clear that the drinks couldn't keep pace with the ideas and I suddenly felt a great relief that the lost battalion of Platonic conversationalists wasn't really lost at all.

Our weekend together took a natural course of intense discussion of all thoughts that percolated in the cauldron of our collective philosophical consciousness. From Plato and Aristotle to

Wittgenstein and Heidegger, we purged our cataracts in order to view Being in the light of these radiant philosophical suns. The discussions were in the spirit of the dialectic, flowing to and fro from one pole of the great *Geist* to the next. We traced the history of this form of philosophical communication, using the mode of communication itself. Although originating in Parmenides, the dialectic would truly take hold with Socrates. The Socratic method of dialogue, the relentless questioning and answering, was thought to create a condition for the revelation of truth—or at least the exposure of falsehood. The ultimate goal was the direct understanding of the Forms, the eternal ideas from which everything derives. This was described poetically in Plato's *Republic:* the shackled man in the cave is suddenly unfettered and sees the deceptive shadows on the wall, as well as the light of the sun outside.

The dialectic was in a state of slumber during the long reign of Aristotelian philosophy and was finally reawakened in Kant's *Critique of Pure Reason.* Kant reintroduced the dialectic in his antinomies. He argued that the antinomies were an inherent phenomenon of metaphysical thinking: given any one argument for a certain metaphysical position (thesis), an equally compelling yet opposite one can be generated (antithesis). Hegel took the antinomies and placed them into a temporal flow. The relationship of thesis to antithesis was not a static property of arguments, but rather the process by which truth unfolded in historical time. There were three moments in a dialectical movement (as popularly described): thesis, giving way to antithesis, with both moments being pulled into a third synthesis. Hegel saw this systematic flow of ideas as dominating the history of philosophy as well as the history of Mind itself.

2.

Germane to my own dissertation was what occurred in the post-Hegelian era. Marx, Kierkegaard, and Nietzsche all attempted to reclaim dialectic as a process that is connected to the existential moment of the individual. The formal transformation is most explicitly developed in Marx, not simply by his inversion of dialectical idealism to materialism, but more importantly by the abolition of the third moment of the dialectical movement—the speculative stage of reason or the synthetic moment. In light of Nietzsche and Kierkegaard, one can see the third moment as a condition that propels movement into a *future*, rather than being centered on the existential concerns of the present and lived moment. Thus, they advocated repetition (Kierkegaard) and recurrence (Nietzsche) rather than a linear dialectical progress. It is also important to note that they considered action and decision as necessary to be propelled from the dialectical antagonism of the first two moments. Taken together, it seems that these three post-Hegelian thinkers eliminated the linear extension of the third moment and attempted to usher in a dialectic oscillation—a process that cycled, repeated, or recurred. It is a strange vibration that somehow catapults someone into an existential, individual, and authentic moment.

There appear to be some fundamental elements of the dialectic: desire, difference, oscillation, and identity. Desire is the affective force that brings the two poles of difference together. Oscillation is the exchange of force between the poles of difference and the result is a point of unity in identification. A metaphor from physics is appropriate: the corona discharge of lightning occurs at a certain voltage of electric field, at which point space loses its normal properties of insulation and acquires the properties of conduction. This is precisely what seemed to happen during the course of our discussion at Café Eckstein: the space between Ted and I no longer separated, but unified.

3.

"It always struck me as odd that Kierkegaard reflected on the Old Testament tale of Abraham and Isaac in *Fear and Trembling*. Where does that fit into to his Christianity?"

"Kierkegaard was a total Jew!"

"On the other hand, he retold the story over and over, speculating on what transpired in Abraham's mind—is that unique to Christian philosophy, a focus not simply on behavior but on the state of mind?"

"You're right, you bastard!"

"*Ja, bitte, noch ein Bier.*"

But how could this unlock a door?

4.

This experience of identity was merely the first inkling that something profound and revolutionary was about to occur. In the hours and days that followed, my understanding of myself and the world was toppled. While I had previously localized my identity to somewhere behind my eyes, I suddenly felt that I was existing as the midst of the world. I was drinking from an inexhaustible existential wellspring from which all truth and, more importantly, all meaning flowed. Although Ted had long since returned to Tübingen, the insights continued to unfold at what seemed to be supraluminal velocities. The first day I came to understand the nature of philosophy. The next I saw eye-to-eye with Christ. The day after the Zen Koans unraveled with ease. Soon all fundamental truths of cosmology were revealed. Space, time, consciousness, experience, melted away—and yet everything nonetheless cohered in a perfect unity. I did not think and therefore did not have angst, but my not-thinking was not the same thing as not-knowing. Miraculously, and yet utterly naturally, my very perception of phenomena was imbued with an intelligence the likes of which I never imagined to exist.

I comported myself with the calm of a prophet. When asked what I had done the evening before, I would reply, "I thought through thought" or "I solved all problems of thought." This was a nonchalant fact of life. We are all Buddhas and Christs, are we not?

5.

On my birth and rebirth

My conception coalesced from the chance mingling of seed and soil.

My birthing was laborious, painful—I too plunged into existence bathed in water, blood, and feces. I too was wrapped in the swaddling clothes of the incidental and the accidental. I too was perpetuated in the temporal.

My birth was as meaningless as yours.

But when my mind became fertile, I gestated in the darkness of a new womb. And when my gestation was complete, I passed through the channel of a new vagina.

As woodflakes showered me, as my creations became manifest, I was reborn. Only then was sawdust revealed as cosmos, only then was I saturated with divine essence.

On my prayer

I reflect now, like this:

Divine experience, within and without, thy essence is beyond name, hallowedness, and shame.

Thou art my eternal kingdom of here and now, where there is neither will nor willer.

Quell my stomach so that my mind may be freely one with you. Help me exist beyond self and other and thus beyond trespass.

May I not cling to the flow of temptation and may I exist beyond the realm of good and evil.

On my death

I died and was born again into eternal life.

But what was my death? And what my rebirth?

Death of the body is final. Those who cling to a life beyond death do not flow in the streams of the divine—they are like children crying to avoid bedtime. Divinity is one with the way of nature, it does not strive to be the exception. Thus can be said of miracles— those of true knowledge wish to be in accord with the Way, not to perform tricks that defy it.

And yet *I* died.

No clinging, *no I*. No thought, *no I*. No ado, *no I*.

On my resurrection

If death of the body is permanent, and resurrection is of the living, how can eternal life be experienced?

What is the essence of the eternal? Is it an infinity of moments that permits existence to flow on forever?

The simple nature of that which is eternal is that it exists outside of time.

Do not conceive of heaven as a "there and then"—"*somewhere* in the sky, *when* I die." If we wish to approach its "location," it must be found through the *here and now*. To create the notion of an infinity of moments devalues the moment in which we now exist. To create the notion of this infinity waiting for us at death divests us of the task of achieving the kingdom in the now. *Through the here and now one will pass to the confluence of past, present, and future.*

On being-in-the-moment

No resurrection of the body, no life flowing on forever. Would my death not therefore be a pathetic spectacle?

But did I not have to die and survive death for your sins? Tell me, what possible relationship could there be between *my death* and *your sins?*

That I would allow myself to die reflects nothing but the implications of my own transcendence:

Being-in-the-moment. *No hand, no nail, no wood.* Being-in-the-moment. *No phantom of past, no specter of future.* Being-in-the-moment. *No attraction to life, no repulsion from death.*

To accept with tranquility the configuration of events that results in death itself is the ultimate reflection of a mind at one with the Way. *Death had been conquered long before the crucifixion.* It is your mind that demands a resurrection for some sense of justice, some sense of understanding—some "sense."

Transcend duality and you have transcended self. Transcend self and you have transcended time. Transcend time and you have transcended death.

All that remains . . . Being-in-the-moment.

On love

Can the flower love the root? Can the stream love the river? Is not such love between the one reflexive and meaningless? If love existed, there must be the distinct entities of the lover and the beloved.

Thus, cease the futile task of trying to love, and turn the mind toward the recognition of unity. If you can grasp this in the fullness of experience, then you have already surpassed the power of love. For remember: as the knowledge of good and evil arose mutually in the garden, so does the existence of love mutually give rise to hate.

As a sage has said:

> The perfect way knows no difficulties
> except that it refuses to make preferences;
> Only when freed from hate and love,
> it reveals itself fully and without disguise

One has commanded: love your neighbor as yourself. Now I command: *no neighbor, no self.*

On faith

No magical birth, no miracle. No resurrection of the body, no life after death. What need is there for faith? What things unseen to be believed?

I once thought that these objects of faith were not to be surpassed, that nothing could be more difficult than this: to believe that God and I are fundamentally different. But there is a task of faith far more difficult: to believe that God and I are fundamentally identical. That divinity is within my capability, that I am pregnant with the eternal, that self-knowledge is knowledge of myself as God.

For all hearts can be anointed and all minds awakened.

6.

In my last days of the experience, I could neither speak nor write. Wittgenstein concluded his revolutionary *Tractatus* with a cryptic aphorism: what we cannot speak about, we must pass over in silence. This misses the mark, for we can speak about only what we *can* pass over. That which is truly ineffable cannot be passed over, nor passed under; we cannot get around it, nor sit beside it. We are not simply *in* the midst of it—we *are* the midst of it.

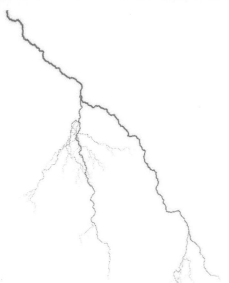

figments and fragments

1.

There was a press release after my scholarship was awarded and the headline read:

"Graduate Student Becomes Dimlit Scholar, Studies Philosophy in Berlin." I felt it would have been appropriate to issue a follow-up story, entitled: "Dimlit Scholar Becomes Buddha, Solves all Problems of Western Thought." Alas, it was not meant to be. One week later, another story emerged: "Buddha Becomes Disturbed Drunk, Contemplates Suicide Daily." Tragically, the experience that I thought would explode into a Swedenborgian mushroom cloud of mysticism had dissipated as rapidly as it had precipitated. It has been said that experiencing *satori* without having studied the sutras is like opening your eyes in a darkened room and that studying the sutras without experiencing *satori* is like turning the light on with your eyes closed. One morning I awoke and realized that I had gone back to sleep: my eyes were again closed in my darkened room. Suddenly, it was me again. Me, me, and *More* me. My existence had become as egocentric as it had been decentralized and all of the thought and commentary that was so gloriously quiescent roared on again with a vengeance. My philosophical muse degenerated into an angry voice that viciously reproached me minute by minute, driving me to obsess about the ultimate act of egocentricity: suicide. The details are rather tedious. Only those who have actually committed suicide have an interesting story to tell—but they tend to be notoriously poor historians.

2.

In *Human, All Too Human*, Nietzsche remarked that for the male sickness of self-contempt, the surest cure is to be loved by a clever woman.[6] Daphne was just that—a clever woman. And, for a brief moment, I was cured. I was awestruck by her beauty when I first saw her standing in the hotel lobby, attending a conference of international graduate students in the spring before I left Berlin. She had traveled to Germany from Seville, where she was conducting a fascinating historical study of a special kind of *paella* made by Flamenco-dancing anarchists during the Spanish Civil War. The moment we met at the opening reception, I could never have imagined that within hours she would capture my heart. I could never have imagined that within weeks we would experience a love of surreal passions and proportions. I could never have imagined that within months she would unlock the Gordian knot of my emotions with her insight. I could never have imagined that, that *fucking bitch*, with her New York pretensions, babbling on about modern dance with those feigned idiosyncrasies that, like everything else about her, were contrived only to form a unique class of which only she was a member, a diaphanous defense against the judgment of her cold critical mother and her distant father, an escape from the contributions of her grandfather and the barons that preceded him, past generations that made her fear competition and comparison, because she knew deep down that she couldn't cut the muster, and *oh, I'm the great dancer who also loves to eat cheeseburgers!* I wouldn't know if she were a great dancer because I never saw her dance, but I did have sex with her and had to force myself to endure her robotic machinations, her eyes wide open like a fish or a corpse, her watching me, her superego watching her, her mother watching her superego, infinitely regressing away from the experience, escaping into mechanistic automatisms, driving me finally to make a sign and protest in Rockefeller Plaza: *"Keep Merce Cunningham Out of My Bedroom!"* And those bastards she called friends? The Bitch Twins? Laurel & Hardy meets Lenny & George meets Homosexuality meets Neurosis? Intolerable assholes. Castor was svelte, almost cachectic, his long hair greased and coiffed. His face was as taut and terse as his personality, with skin stretched tightly over a bony architecture like some congenital facelift. His brother Pollux, on the other hand, was a corpulent, diaphoretic buffoon. He constantly had a cigarette in his hand and cocaine in his brain, both of which generated an overwrought energy that spilled out in the form of "shocking" vulgarity and painfully contrived monologue that usually degenerated into soliloquy. Their stark diametrical opposition pointed unambiguously to a common origin and they were, indeed, both poisoned fruits sprouting from the same diseased tree. Only two individuals in close relation can mutually define each other as such antitheses. During my time in New York, Castor was clearly dealing with the loss of his father by using control, compulsion, and insurmountable barriers to intimacy. His hypersensitivity to abandonment made him territorially pissy about Daphne in a queer passive-aggressive way and he clearly feared the loss of another loved one, this time to a heterosexual lover—a fate worse than death. While Castor concealed, Pollux revealed. The tent of his three-ring circus personality only thinly veiled the proverbial tears of the clown. He acted-out to ever more ridiculous levels, offering me fellatio and cocaine virtually every time I saw him. The three of them wallowed in a hurt that eluded them and their despair was often misdirected at their admittedly mediocre artistic careers. That *fucking bitch.*

3.

How did that just happen? How did the beginning of a love story unleash such venom? I wanted to tell the tale of how we first met . . .

"It's a pleasure to meet you, Daphne. Was your name taken from the work of Ovid?"

"Yes, precisely."

"I translated the work from Latin in high school."

. . . and go on to describe that magical April in Seville, the festival, the Flamenco dancers, the white shaded space of the apartment, the cold Spanish sherry, the hot Danish neighbor, the blistering yellow sun on the blue-tiled roof, the succulent oranges, the invitation to live in New York after Berlin, the flowing conversations, the deep joy, the phrase that I could not suppress, the words that battled their way out of my mouth against my will: *I love you.* How could I shamelessly go on to call her a witch with a capital B? How did that just happen?

I suppose the deeper question is how that happens in any relationship. How do we start out in loving intimacy with one individual and end up in bitter estrangement from another? It seems appropriate to introduce an important concept from the philosophy of science, the concept of *paradigm shift*. Thomas Kuhn wrote a book in the early 1960s entitled *The Structure of Scientific Revolutions* in which he argued against the slow, stepwise, rational accretion of scientific knowledge and instead put forth the theory that quantum jumps and discontinuities drive science through the process of paradigm shifts. A paradigm is a certain kind of scientific *Weltanschauung*, or worldview. It is used as a lens through which to view natural phenomena and as a guide to formulate further hypotheses and experimentation. Consider the Ptolemaic *geocentric* paradigm, which asserted that the sun revolves around the earth. Through this, astronomers had certain guiding assumptions about the heavens, assumptions that turned out to be wrong. The elucidation of this error, however, came through the radical break of the Copernican revolution, or the *heliocentric* paradigm—the notion that the earth revolves around the sun. At a certain point of scientific research, enough *counterinstances* of the geocentric paradigm occurred to hit a critical point in which the theory broke down and could be replaced by another. It may sometimes be the case that the data remain the same, while only the explanation or abductive reasoning about the data is different. It is remarkable that the community of scientists can at one point think of the sun as revolving around the earth and at another think of the earth revolving around the sun.

But isn't that precisely what happens to us in relationships?

On Wednesday somebody is spontaneous and on Thursday impulsive. The boyfriend who just last week was free-spirited is now undisciplined. The woman who was thought to be emotionally expressive is suddenly regarded as a petulant child. As if by black magic, all of the qualities that were viewed within the paradigm of *love* precipitously come to be viewed within the paradigm of *hatred, contempt,* or *sheer indifference.* It is somewhat like looking at an optical illusion. One moment there is a vase awaiting red roses and the next there are two faces screaming at each other. One longs to pet the ears of the adorable bunny rabbit, but suddenly realizes it is the parted beak of a duck poised to snip one's penis off.

There are different ways this can happen. One way is that new data can be collected that represent a critical counterinstance of the paradigm. For example, a wife opens the drawer of her husband's workbench in order to retrieve a screwdriver and ends up retrieving a negligee, a wig, and a latex strap-on. The wife in this example may sense that it is time to formulate a new framework within which to view the behavioral data of her husband. Another way that a relational paradigm shift can occur is by viewing the same data in a completely new light. In this instance, data that were recognized but excluded from the paradigm begin to assert themselves repeatedly and in an incontrovertible fashion. The woman who is about to divorce an adulterous man is shocked and indignant about his lack of commitment—even though she started sleeping with him while he was married to his third wife. The data that were present and in fact integral to the development of the relationship were once ignored, but now come to dominate the new paradigm. The first type of relational paradigm shift can be devastating: looking back, one feels as if one has been living a lie and develops a profound hatred for the person who has concealed the crucial information. But the second case is far worse—there is no one to blame but yourself. The data were always there, right before your eyes: you recognized them, but failed to make them a part of your narrative.

Kuhn discusses the phenomenon of resistance to the paradigm shift. He posits that it is in the nature of the scientific community to resist acceptance of the new worldview. Science is a conservative and skeptical endeavor and the scientist is (in the modernist view) the gatekeeper to the realm of fact. Thus, there cannot be an uncritical reception of the shifting paradigm and the scientist must attempt to explain the data through the pre-existing paradigm to the extent that it is possible. In the case of the shift from Newtonian physics to quantum physics, Max Planck, who first recognized the quanta or packets of energy through the phenomenon of black body radiation, was repulsed by his own findings. He himself was so accustomed to the classical paradigm of continuous energy distribution that he could hardly tolerate the prospect that it could be wrong. In losing a paradigm, one does not simply lose a set of data, but rather loses a way of viewing the world—which is tantamount in some cases to losing the world itself.

What is seen as resistance in the scientific community is often manifested as denial in the individual. The paradigm shift of a relationship is often accompanied by the angst of a lost world and there is thus only a reluctant acceptance of it. Like the scientist, the individual attempts to view the new and disturbing phenomena in the light of the pre-existing worldview. Consider the latex strap-on, for example. This is absurd, he couldn't possibly take pleasure in this, this ungodly filth. Him dressing up and then somebody driving this monstrosity deep into his, his . . . no, this is simply not possible. Well, for the love of God, what *else* could he be using it for? I found it in the workbench, right? So maybe he uses it as some type of tool—and after all he is quite a talented handyman, isn't he? Yes, a *tool* of some kind! It has a hole at the tip, so perhaps it's a dispenser of sorts, a dispenser that allows his hands to be free for other activities. Yes, *exactly,* it's autumn and he usually caulks the windows again for winter! I bet he uses both hands to hold the curtains back while this device delivers the caulking to the windows! And . . . *of course!* He wants to be creative and efficient in his work, but doesn't want to look strange standing in the window with this thing dribbling caulking like a gonorrheal penis and so *he wears a wig and negligee in order to disguise himself!* That absolute *prince* of a man! To risk shame and humiliation in order to keep me and the children warm all winter—and all without dirtying the curtains? Why, I simply *adore* him!

4.

It is never simply two people who love each other, but two worlds. Although we may sometimes feel like it, we are never lovers floating in a vacuum of space. Lovers must always be seen against their horizon, their background. How many times does a passionate affair during a vacation disintegrate after returning home? How many times do lovers separate after experiencing each other's family—either the family living in the world, or the family living in the head? True love must always coalesce within a certain context, an authentic context of each individual. But what does *true* love mean? Was the love between Daphne and me any less true because it did not last? Is *durability* the criterion of truth when it comes to love? Or is it a particular quality or intensity that defines the truth of love? Whatever the answer, the romantic horizon of Seville could not fit within the crowded horizon of New York. It became clear within weeks that our two worlds would not fit into one. I felt a deep sense of loss—or rather, *a deep sense of loss was revealed*. I realized that I could not continue in this state. I did not want to indulge in my depressed emotions like a whimpering child, so I did the mature thing: I had an affair.

5.

Meeting Dolores in a bookstore near Columbia University was a surprisingly lively encounter. She was perusing a book by Lyotard when, stealthily, I approached her and introduced myself.

"Yes, hello Dorian, I'm Dolores Hayes." She returned immediately to her book, patently annoyed. I was not deterred.

"Dolores Haze, as in the Dolores Haze from Nabokov?"

She rolled her eyes in irritation. "Yes, precisely—but don't even think of calling me Lolita, you asshole."

Wounded, but not fatally so, I pressed on.

"Oddly enough, I once translated *Lolita* from the original and . . ."

She slammed the book down and glowered. "Oh, you translated *Lolita* from the original, did you? Well that is *quite* an accomplishment, Dorian, especially considering that Nabokov wrote the original in *English*, you asshole!"

I was briefly tempted to respond with "Well, no wonder it was so damned easy!" but I wasn't about to let this young vixen get the best of me quite yet. Noting her interest in Lyotard, I knew where best to strike—and vowed never again to reference literature while meeting women in a bookstore.

"I didn't translate it from *English*, you insouciant little minx! I translated it from its *modernity*, from the rationalist presuppositions of the Enlightenment. I masterfully extracted the grand metanarrative and, like a deconstructive Samurai warrior, sliced it into a plethoric multiplicity of non-consensual Wittgensteinian language games, serving it with a neostructuralist parsley to a stunned audience at the École Normale. I sée you're reading Lyotard—in *English*? *Mon Dieux!* Jean-Francois was thére, Mademoiselle Haze, and hé wept tears of joy as I made a deft and near-perilous hermeneutic rescue of *Lolita* from its Cartesian prison, liberating it into a post-modern experiment known only as Lo.Li. Ta. I'll bé damned if I didn't gaze into the crowd to find Derrida répositioning an érection. *Ach*, but what would you know, you, you ... *Frankfurt schoolgirl.* I took one look at your shoes and said to myself, *pure Habermas. Guten Abend, mademoiselle, und au revoir.*" I love post-modernity—it's what I talk about when I have nothing left to say.

We met for dinner, my tirade having convinced her that I was no asshole—at least no ordinary asshole. I described by upcoming plans to attempt a practical experiment in philosophy. I would work in a psychiatry ward at Harvard Medical School and relate the work of Nietzsche to Freud, as a *living* philosopher. She announced that she was a writer, a novelist in fact, but had not yet started her first novel because of her heavy coursework at Columbia. I met many such people in New York: writers who hadn't published a pamphlet, dancers who couldn't tap their feet in a disco, fashion designers who hadn't sold a pair of socks. All of them superciliously insisted, however, that they were *writers, dancers,* and *designers.* Running in these circles filled me with great regret. I realized that as a conventional well-published scholar, I was in the unfortunate situation of having actualized too much potential. They made me yearn for the state of pure possibility such that I, too, could brandish my nothingness with an edgy arrogance—a blade never dulled on the concrete of reality.

Upon further reflection, though, I *didn't* think of myself as a scholar, but rather as a philosopher—and what right did I have to do so? As a graduate student, I had not written books, nor made any significant contribution to the field. I suppose it was because philosophy was the activity in which I felt most myself and most connected to the world. Do writers have to publish in order to call themselves writers? Do writers require critical acceptance or popularity in order to call themselves writers? Or do writers simply have to write passionately? On the one hand, it is a matter of identity, a matter of subjectivity. On the other hand, there seems to be a value in publication, quite literally, in making something public. Where does the state of being a writer exist: in the head of the writer, or in the head of the reader? It must be somewhere in between, for otherwise we are left with the unappealing choices of solipsism or behaviorism.

We have a narrative of ourselves just as we have a paradigm of our relationships. We extract the data of our being and construct a story of the self, a story such as "philosopher" or "writer." Nietzsche appreciated the role of lies and omissions in such narratives, perhaps because of his belief that there were no facts, but merely interpretations. This thinking was called "Perspectivism," the assertion that there was no one Truth, but rather a variety of perspectives. The view of modernism is that various perspectives of rational thought are incomplete descriptions of one underlying reality. What Nietzsche was saying was quite different, however: there is no *underlying* reality because *reality is nothing but the perspective itself.* The defining mark of "post-modernity" is that just as there can be no "underlying reality" there can also be no "overlying narrative," or *metanarrative.* Metanarratives were attempts to capture reality with one grand schema, such as Freud's psychoanalysis or Marx's concept of class conflict or Hegel's dialectic. When approaching the Truth, we are left with several choices: 1) going the way of the Enlightenment and adopting a grand metanarrative, 2) developing a post-modern comfort with many discrete and equally valid narratives, or 3) arriving at a consensus of disparate discourses through dialogue, the approach of Jürgen Habermas and the Frankfurt School.

Is the same true for the narratives and perspectives of the self? Am I condemned to my figments and fragments, am I damned to a mosaic of selves? Can there truly be no metanarrative that brings them all together, nor any one substance from which they all flow? Can there ever be a consensus of the many selves within? And if so, is this watered-down average of agreement something desirable? I was weary from questions and Dolores was cradled in my arms, her eyes falling heavy as she descended into the labyrinths. Her face was smooth and placid from the wine and sex, and she looked much younger than when I met her in the bookstore. She smiled in a somnolent delirium while murmuring the last words of the day and I kissed her forehead tenderly and whispered:

"Sweet dreams . . . *Lolita.*"

6.

I was leaving New York the week of my thirtieth birthday. It was a strange time to be with strangers, but then again I didn't really have any friends. As I approached my natal anniversary, I appreciated that my physical being was in the throes of change. I was hovering in a unique state between the teen-age process of acne and the middle-age process of balding. There was an unfortunate relationship between the two. Sadly, the follicles that once grew hair started growing oil instead, leaving my forehead with a shine that would turn any black Italian loafer green with envy. Soon I discovered the myth of hair loss and realized the yet more frightening reality of hair redistribution. I have yet to fathom the cruel evolutionary logic that makes a man lose hair on his head, then gain it on his shoulders, back, earlobes, and nostrils. The change of identity was disturbing, even frightening, until I realized that it was not I who was dying, but merely my curly-haired narrative. Another story would always emerge.

Daphne decided to have a dinner party to celebrate my birthday—and my departure. There were many artists, writers, and critics in attendance, and, of course, the Bitch Twins. I must admit that I was having difficulty following most of the discussions and was shocked to realize that this could even be possible after years of such intense scholarship. When it came to literature, my mind's eye simply had no powers of resolution. Between elucidating the structure of reality and chasing women, I had always been far too busy to read fiction or appreciate culture. Daphne was *mortified*. I thought E.M. Forster wrote *Out of Africa* rather than *A Passage to India*. They are both very poor countries, are they not? I said George Orwell when I meant George Eliot—but who can blame me for confusing these two great men of literature? When asked my thoughts on Saki, I knowledgeably replied that I preferred it cold to hot, but when dining Japanese usually drank Sapporo. *Kampai!*

Meanwhile, Daphne was droning on about how *faaah-bulous* modern *dahnce* was. The way she spoke about Isadora and José, Merce and Martha, I thought they were couples living in her apartment building. I found her speaking with an aspiring dance critic. His rotund girth was approaching the circumference of a small asteroid and I suspected he had difficulty seeing his feet, let alone moving them gracefully. It has been said that critics are like eunuchs in a harem. How true it is: they can see it being done, they can talk about who does it well, but they simply can't do it themselves.

He pulled me aside and cooed, "For someone trained in modern, Daphne really has one of the best Attitudes I have ever seen."

"Really? I think she has become an intolerable snob."

Daphne was becoming *furioso* with me and hit me right where it hurt. I become livid, paralyzed with anger when I recall what she said. Right at the dinner table! In front of *everyone!* In front of . . . *company!*

"Dorian is a person of such . . . *decency*."

That frigid monster! What unmitigated temerity! How *dare* she!

"How *dare* you, you frigid monster!" I bellowed in my head, imagining how ashen their faces would have turned if I had actually said something. "*I am just as depraved as any of you!*"

I bit my tongue until it was blood-red, grabbed the chair beneath me until my knuckles were bone-white. I was tired of New York. I was tired of talking, tired of talk. I calmed myself with the knowledge that in mere days I would arrive in Boston and was already grateful to be back in an environment more sympathetic to my philosophical inclinations.

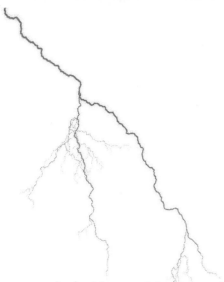

shrinking at harvard

1.

"Eternal fucking *what?* Jeeesus H. Christ!"

Dr. Quirky, my mentor at Harvard, was not exactly sympathetic to my philosophical inclinations. Short and trim with olive skin and a Roman nose, his eyelids fell half-mast as his lower jaw jutted forth in contempt.

"This is a fucking hospital, not a college dorm. Think what you want, but don't let me hear any of that Nietzsche bullshit while we are rounding on patients!"

My ingenious experiment of the living philosopher in the clinic seemed to be withering on the vine. I walked around in shock, frightened and disturbed by the zombies leaning against the pale yellow walls. Spaced-out, glassy-eyed, tie-dyed, and bell-bottomed, they seemed to have stepped out of a time capsule from the early 1970s. More troubling yet, most of them were staff.

"You will attend morning rounds. You will listen to my lectures. You will interview patients. You will attend personal therapy sessions with our psychologist Dr. Hilton. You will be on call once a week. You will not be a pain in my ass!"

I was torn between a military salute and a simple "Yes, Papa."

"Nurse Leoni! Get your fat black ass out of that chair and show our young . . . doc-tor" (he drew the word out in disgust) "where the call room is!"

Irritated, I explained that the term doctor is, in fact, an academic title and that physicians have merely professional rather than scholarly training.

His response: a shrug of the shoulders and a "What-the-fuck-ever."

Nurse Leoni was in fact fat, black, and nothing short of beautiful mother love incarnate. With a bright smile, her plump sausage arm miraculously telescoped around me to grab my shoulder warmly.

"Now don't you go a-worryin', Dr. Dorian," she soothed in a Jamaican tongue, "dat ol' Dr. Quirky get ugly wit' EVeryone!"

"Goddammit Leoni! Just show him where the fucking call room is!"

There was a pause, and then the room shook:

"Don't you take the Lord's name in vain!"

A sonic boom. A mountain being born. A volcano erupting. A glacier collapsing. A selection of In-a-Gadda-Da-Vida on the hydrogen jukebox. We trembled in silence. Two staff members scurried from the room gobbling pilfered Valium. Three patients instantaneously began to cry.

"I'm sorry Ms. Leoni." Quirky earnestly whined, boyish and effeminate. He was predisposed to pushing buttons, but didn't realize that this particular one would detonate a nuclear warhead.

What a scene: contempt, tenderness, blasphemy, rage, fear, supplication! What an oasis after years of hearing phrases such as ". . . let me contextualize this problematic for you by proffering an ontologic language game on an epistemologic horizon. . . ." This talk, these people seemed real . . . but what does that really mean?

2.

My first night "on call," the euphemism for the overnight slave labor of resident physicians, was a harsh awakening from the Ivory Tower. My responsibility was to "shadow" the resident, observing her as she evaluated incoming patients and solved the emergent problems of patients in the locked ward. The problems presenting throughout the night were an assortment of rotten candy in a year-old gift box, each bite assaulting the palate more than the last: the cherry cordial of mania, the half-bitter chocolate of depression, the nutty maple cream of schizophrenia. As with all other aspects of life, drugs and alcohol muddied the waters. Was this patient intoxicated, or was he merely withdrawing? Had drug abuse caused her psychosis, or was she self-medicating the disease?

Despite my lack of medical training, the patients nonetheless referred to me as "Doc."

"Can I have a smoke, Doc?"

"What time is it, Doc?"

"Can you buy me a soda, Doc?"

"I'm going to hunt you down in Boston and chop off your balls, Doc."

As Dr. Quirky wryly noted earlier that day, it is twice as hard to look half as normal in a psychiatric hospital. Thus, at 2:00 a.m., when I saw Mrs. Balducci screaming *"DOC!* My son abandoned me and now I have the holy blood of a Long Island Jesus spurting forth from my ass!" I naturally thought she was crazy. Mrs. B. was nervously shuffling toward us in the hall, pale as a ghost, but then suddenly stopped to remove her hospital gown: spreading her legs and closing her eyes, she proceeded to gush bright red bloody shit all over the floor, her palms facing forward in anticipation of stigmata.

"Oh my God," mumbled the resident through the hand covering her mouth, "she has a G.I. bleed. This is an emergency—her blood pressure can bottom out in minutes."

A complex set of events was set into motion that ultimately led to the transfer of the patient to the neighboring General Hospital. I was left to clean up the mess while the resident slept. I had spent many late nights with alcohol and women, but when the alcohol was used to sterilize the floor and the woman was a schizophrenic septuagenarian painting Jackson Pollocks with her hemorrhaging asshole, I knew I had turned a corner in life.

3.

Punch-drunk with sleep deprivation, I arrived the next morning at the office of Dr. Sarah Hilton, the psychodynamic psychotherapist at the hospital. Her office was a respite from the depressing hues of the jaundiced institutional walls. There were sunflowers and ferns, Picasso lithographs, oriental rugs, mahogany-framed degrees, books, books, books, and, of course, *the couch.* I offered to shake her hand, but instead she simply extended it toward the plush altar of therapy . . .

"MR. ALEXANDER!"

I had fallen asleep only five minutes into the session.

"Tell me the first things that come to mind when I say *mother* and *father*."

"Oh, you must be joking!"

Again, with precisely the same hoity-Freudy intonation, "Tell me the first things that come to mind when I say *mother* and *father*."

Half-asleep, I am suddenly back in their Cambridge apartment in the late 1960s, present, but somehow older than both of them. Karl has a noose around his neck and is hanging from the rafters above. His face is becoming blue and contorted and he is both desperately trying to loosen the knot as well as swing into the nearby fan in the hope that it will sever the rope. Helen is lying in bed laughing at the sight of this, her naked body brown and hot from the Greek sun that she had recently absorbed.

"Nothing, really."

"*Nothing* comes to your mind when I say *mother* and *father*?!" The emotional valence betrayed her inexperience.

I am in bed with Helen, massaging olive oil into her breasts and tasting the fullness of her lips as we begin to make love. She wets my ear with her tongue and whispers in Ancient Greek "*You are fucking your mother—when she was younger than you!*"

"No, nothing is really coming to mind." Why make it easy for her?

We *are* fucking and it is incredible. She seems to be easing in and out of time, from her late teens to her mid-twenties and as I lean down to kiss her breasts, they become for an instant prepubescent, transforming again to their womanly fullness within a blink of the mind's eye. Karl, in the meantime, is swinging from the rafters, dead and exsanguinating from every pore and orifice. The whirling fan is spraying a hot bloody mist over our naked bodies and, as we near orgasm, the most amazing thing happens: the blades of the fan, sharpened to a razor's edge on the philosopher's stone of my id, sever father's head clean off, sending it and his decapitated body plummeting to the floor with a fantastic *THUMP-THUMP*. Tears fall from his eyes as they stare at his body beside him, while Helen and I shriek in ecstasy, the hills of Elysium themselves filling our voices. We begin to pass a strange event horizon: space is turning black and time slows down, every second expanding toward our mutual climax. As we begin to tremble and convulse, I am finally able to ask: "Why did you kill yourself?"

"Oh, my darling Dorian," she sweetly replies, wiping currant-jelly clots from her bloodied lips, "*because I love you!*"

4.

My impressions about psychiatry, and in particular psychoanalysis, were misguided: what I thought was a cerebral and philosophical discipline was in fact dedicated to *emotional space*. Despite his rough-hewn persona, Quirky was clearly dedicated to the education of the residents, interns, and graduate students. During his lectures on psychoanalysis, he allowed me to give the first talk on Nietzsche, acknowledging Freud's debt to the master. Indeed, Nietzsche's discussions of the narrow domain of conscious thought, as well as his keen understanding of repression, lies, and memories, laid the foundation for the analytic principles of Freud. Freud once stated that Nietzsche possessed a nobility to which he could not even aspire and suggested that Nietzsche had greater powers of introspection than anyone in history. Oh, Nietzsche—why *are* you a destiny?

Dr. Quirky continued, discussing Freud's structural theory of mind, the intrapsychic conflicts that lead to repression and censorship, then dream interpretation, the royal road to the unconscious. Sigmund Freud, however, was only the beginning of a rich history of psychoanalysis. Anna Freud continued the work, recognizing that the ego has a number of strategies with which to avoid intolerable emotions and further associated these defense mechanisms with various psychopathologies. Psychic disorders, however, do not simply result from internal conflicts in an isolated being. Klein and Winnicott developed theories that explore our initial relationships to various "objects"—people (such as mommies) and things (such as blankies) to which we are bound. The processes of attachment and separation are crucial in the development of the healthy psyche. Their disorders can lead to a hypersensitivity to loss and abandonment, an unstable sense of self, and an insatiable "object hunger," where the object can be anybody or anything that brings comfort and security to the moment. Finally, Quirky described the "self-psychology" of Heinz Kohut, as well as a bevy of other theories that extended into post-modernity.

With these tools, I was able to engage in a primitive form of analysis within my first days of interviewing. The patients were afflicted with various complex pathologies that, more often than not, were initiated by early insults and abuses. The question of mind and brain became futile: the feedback mechanisms and interdigitations of the "psychic" and "physical" processes left the dichotomy all but meaningless. As physicists map forces in Euclidean or Riemannian space, so do analysts map the emotional space, searching for clues in conversation and observation that elucidate the motivations driving us to construct behaviors that defend against intolerable affects. The question is, of course, how to break the patterns. As Nietzsche stated: "The will to overcome an affect is ultimately only the will of another, or several affects."[7] This was often true: the Freudian "talking cure" was not enough. Insights were important, but replacing and restructuring emotional and cognitive structures in therapy were often the key to health. Nonetheless, conversation seemed to play a crucial role, the dialectic again at work. This oscillation seemed to shake up and break up ossified psychic patterns. "Breaking up"—isn't that really what the "lysis" in "analysis" means? The process of analysis was a series of breaks and the breakthroughs were *initiated* by the breakdowns, not cures to counteract them.

5.

I was guilt-ridden that I had been giving Dr. Hilton too little for her efforts in my early sessions and so I lay upon the couch again with a firm resolve to be a more productive analysand. For each of her investigations, I intended to deliver full satisfaction.

"Dorian, what are you *feeling* right now?"

"I feel, I feel . . . I feel *younger* somehow."

"Interesting. Tell me more."

"I feel, I feel . . . I feel as if I am a *boy* again."

"Really. And how do you *feel* about that?"

"I feel, I feel . . . I feel as if I want to *fuck you.*"

"Yes, yes, interesting. Now tell me, Dorian: when you *feel* like you want to fuck me, who do you *feel* that I am?"

"I feel, I feel . . . I feel as if you are *my mommy*."

"Yes, Dorian, in a way I *am* mommy right now. And tell me, what does mommy *feel* like?"

"W-wait . . . m-me getting younger now."

"You getting younger now?"

"Pee-pee maker feel funny, feel different."

"Yes, tell me 'bout *pee-pee maker*."

"Pee-pee maker get hard."

"Yes, interesting, but how does that make you *feel* right now."

"Me want suck mommy."

"You want suck mommy?"

"Me want sucky-suck."

"And would you like mommy to suck hard pee-pee maker?"

"Me don't care no more 'bout pee-pee maker."

"Yes, indeed! You don't care 'bout pee-pee maker no more! Now you want sucky-sucky!"

Dr. Hilton was clearly not aware that most advanced graduate students in philosophy have at least a passing familiarity with Freud's theory of psychosexual development. Unfortunately, on a crash course of regression from the Oedipal to the genital to the oral, I realized that I had failed to pluck that puckered rosebud of our common psychic ancestry. I had to save face—and fast.

"I feel, I feel . . . I feel bottom funny."

"Yes! *Yes!* How bottom *feel?*" She was so enthralled I thought she would mount me on the couch for a lesson in lay analysis.

"Backside poo-poo maker feel tingly."

"Does poo-poo maker want make poo-poo, Dorian?"

I sensed we were on the verge of a profound insight, so it was time to up the ante. "*Mommy always get MAD if I make poo-poo!*"

"*NO*, Dorian, NO! Mommy will *not* be mad. Mommy *loves* you."

"O.K. make poo-poo?"

"*O.K. make poo-poo, Dorian. O.-K.*"

"Goo goo ga ga."

Never one to be a tease, I knew it was time to consummate our journey to the center of the mind. I knew it was time . . . to make poo-poo.

"Yes, Dorian," she sniffed in the air like a dog. "*Oh, my God, YES!* Good boy! *Good boy*, Dorian."

I felt the hot wet paste of a therapeutic breakthrough covering my buttocks and thighs.

"Oh, dear, but I am afraid our time is up."

I snapped to attention. "Yes, of course Dr. Hilton, it is important that we not transgress any boundaries that might confound the transference."

"Precisely, you are quite insightful."

"The terminus was indeed serendipitous, Dr. Hilton—my regression was entering the pre-natal state. I felt as if I would imminently become the cellular raspberry from which we all develop."

"An *excellent* goal for next session Dorian!"

6.

As the months passed, the essential relevance of the psychiatric experience was becoming manifest to me. Although I was far from the eternal recurrence of the present, I was in close proximity to witness and record the eternal recurrence of the *past*. The victims of abuse were a sad example of this. Often assaulted from within the womb by alcohol and drugs, these children grew up as objects used for beatings and rapes by parents who may have been psychiatrically impaired themselves. While other organisms retain a deep memory and aversive response to noxious stimuli, human beings sadly seem ever to return to them. Thus, the children of abuse grow to re-engage in drugs, prostitution, and the assault of their own children. The haunted past seemed always to return.

Those with neurosis allowed me to gain great insight into the eternal recurrence of the *past*. The neurotic personality is impotent in the face of the present moment because it almost invariably returns to an earlier time. Like a large funnel, the neurotic mind collects the droplets of perception and experience and directs them to the same narrow tube of the repressed emotion. Fortunately, there are events that may fall outside of the collecting basin of this structure, but the more profound the neurosis, the broader the diameter of the funnel. Whatever comes to the mind in the present moment becomes transformed to its distant relative in the past, so that the associated emotions that were never allowed to be experienced can finally breathe again. This is how the relationship with girlfriend becomes the relationship with mother, or how the rude man at work becomes the alcoholic father leaving home all over again. Locked up in a past that was never allowed to be a present, neurosis abuses our moments by using them to give voice to emotions that were always silenced. The problem is not that you recollect your past, but rather that your past recollects you.

With each new experience missed as it falls into the funnel of the past, the psyche often tries to recapture the moment with other compensatory mechanisms: fantasy, delusion, or psychosis. Fantasy could take the form of future dreams or imaginations, or could be the more subtle fantasy that veils the true meaning of a moment. With the present simply becoming a battlefield between neurosis and fantasy, one becomes condemned to an eternal recurrence of the past or a recurrent projection of the future, a life that consists of "thens" and "yet to comes."

During the months of my experiences with Dr. Hilton, a method emerged for the madness. My relationship with her became the canvas on which the unresolved emotions of the past could finally be painted. Not by doing, but rather by being-with, she enabled the muted voices to speak. Hidden emotions were not simply thought about, but experienced, and with them the source of many behaviors became revealed. How much of my thinking, how much of my behavior was merely a sophisticated escape, an escape from simply being in the moment with my emotions? In therapy, I felt more like Dorian Gray than Dorian Alexander. The hidden canvas on which I painted so many ugly emotions was suddenly before my eyes, allowing me an understanding of why the narrow scope of my daily consciousness was so unflappable, so unassailable. I saw the many canvases of my self, all hidden from one another in an abandoned museum, a silent space where no one including me was allowed. Suddenly, I felt myself shrinking: not just my problems, but the very structure of my past. With the past no longer poised to attack the present, I could approach each moment not as an eternal recurrence but as *new*. With the needs of the past shrinking, so did the needs of the future. Slowly, each moment began to expand, no longer encroached upon by the just-thens and the yet-to-comes.

7.

"Tell me about the corals, Dorian."

I described my timeless descent into the black-lit waters, the gentle fall to the spongy nexus from which these elegant creatures burst forth.

"What were they to you, Dorian?"

The feminine. The feminine that seemed always to live, to create life, and to support life even from the porous remnants of its own corpse. I saw the feminine that gave birth to something real and that nurtured even in death. I saw it next to the porous remnants of lava, the mark of the masculine: molten, unpredictably belligerent, erupting in frustration, inexorably flowing forth, burning and petrifying, leaving hollowness and death in its wake.

"Why did you first see them, Dorian?"

The memories and emotions poured over me: the anguished screams, the shrieking of shattered glass, the curses of "I hate you," the violence of slammed doors and broken commitments, the fear, the isolation, the instinct to protect, the weakness, the failure, the confusing silence of the aftermath, the tears of rage and shame, all slowly muted as I became transfixed by the gurgle-gurgle and whoosh-whoosh of the aquarium, the forgetful waters of the Lethe, the Styx of drugs and sex, the Dead Sea of thought and time, the final swamp of nothingness, the ultimate perversion: Philosophy.

sons of the father

1.

It is of interest to speculate on the origins of Nietzsche's fervor in his struggle against Christ and the Christian, and important to note the loss of his own father—a Lutheran minister—at an early age. This loss—in conjunction with his exquisite sensitivity and intellectual conscience, his gentle mannerisms, his physical frailty—leads one to question whether his philosophy was more of a personal fantasy rather than a cultural or existential vision. Was Nietzsche's fervent stance as anti-Christ nothing more than a reaction against the severity of his own superego, which, as Freud notes, is a longing for the father? He claimed that Christianity was the revenge of the weak against the strong, a phantasm of those who needed another world because of their failure in this one. Perhaps Nietzsche, the "philosopher of the future," was even weaker—not only did he need a new religion, but also needed himself to be the God. Did Nietzsche suffer from a God complex, as suggested by the psychoanalyst Ernest Jones? This obsession with Christianity and Christ, this "God is dead," was it all nothing more than the pathetic cry of a little boy, the pathetic little cry of *"I miss you, Daddy"*?

2.

Nietzsche wrote that if a son does not have a good father, he should furnish himself with one. *Schopenhauer und Wagner*? He also wrote that fathers have much to do to make amends for having sons. In order to complete my dissertation, I would have to investigate Nietzsche's son—the teacher of the eternal recurrence.

Nietzsche never married, although he did make clumsy proposals to the alluring Lou Salomé, a free spirit and prominent intellectual who rejected him twice. Nietzsche did, however, have a child—his own gift to the world of men—and his name was *Zarathustra*. Zarathustra's name was Latinized to become Zoroaster, after which the religion Zoroastrianism is named, a religion that asserts the near equal balance of good and evil gods. Zarathustra was the protagonist of Nietzsche's work *Thus Spoke Zarathustra*, an innovative literary-philosophical treatise published in four parts. Zarathustra, who had retreated to the mountains at the age of thirty, has descended ten years later to share his insight with the people. Zarathustra is clearly presented as a quasi-religious figure and delivers speeches that oftentimes reveal a formal—if not substantive—unity with those of Christ. Nietzsche gave us his only son Zarathustra and by doing so felt he had "given mankind the greatest present that has ever been made to it so far." Oh, Nietzsche: why *do* you write such good books?

3.

What of Christ, the son of the Father—and what of his mirror image, Oedipus? Christ and Oedipus stand as two mythical kings, with a remarkable relationship to one another. From birth to death, there are a number of striking parallels and anti-parallels. Both Oedipus and Christ were born under unique circumstances, with the identity of their parents cloaked in obscurity. Oedipus was taken away from his parents in order to thwart infanticide and the Oracle's prophecy that he would slay his father and lay with his mother. Thus was it unknown to Oedipus that his father and mother were king and queen of Thebes. The identity of Christ's parents was also obscured and in a similar fashion it was initially unknown that Christ's father was the King of Kings, and his mother the Holiest of Holy. Oedipus and Christ were both unwitting heirs to a throne and each was destined for a unique kingdom.

Christ and Oedipus ultimately developed an anti-parallel relationship to their parents: their respective triads were diametrically opposed. The father of Oedipus realized his mortality at the hands of his son and his mother Iocaste subsequently had a directly sexual relationship with him. The father of Christ, however, was immortal, and his mother was virginal despite her conception and delivery. Oedipus destroyed the father and achieved union with the mother, while Christ shunned the mother and achieved union with the father. Oedipus destroyed the will of the father in order to inherit his kingdom, while Christ acquiesced to the will of the father in order to inherit his. Oedipus accomplished a worldly kingdom by the assertion of his will, while Christ accomplished a spiritual kingdom by the renunciation of his. We can observe that even the conclusions of each myth are anti-parallel. Oedipus was ultimately punished for affirming his will, while Christ achieved immortality for the renunciation of his. Christ and Oedipus therefore appear in a state of dialectical antagonism with respect to one another.

4.

In many ways, Oedipus and Zarathustra stand in opposition to Christ, but what is their relationship to one other? Is there some order to the triad of Christ, Oedipus, and Zarathustra? During the course of writing my dissertation, I developed the theory that these three personae bore a triadic relationship to one another that represents the three spiritual metamorphoses introduced in the prologue of *Thus Spoke Zarathustra*. In the prologue, Nietzsche describes three metamorphoses of the spirit, which take the form of the camel, the lion, and the child. The strength and the role of the camel is to bear the burden of old values—it acquiesces to the value system to which it is heir. The first metamorphosis transforms the camel into a lion, who proves victorious in the battle against tradition's value-laden dragon. The dragon is described as being covered with scales that read "thou shalt," while the lion battles with the "I will." By conquering the dragon, the lion can only create a condition for the creation of new values, but is incapable of creating value itself. This is the task of the allegorical child, who looks upon life anew and is able to be the creator of new values.

It is likely that the camel is representative of the Christian (if not Christ himself), who, in Nietzsche's perspective, accepts and bears the yoke of slave morality, as well as the mediocre culture of empathy and pity. Nietzsche calls, ironically, for a move *forward* to the pre-Christian and pre-Socratic value schema and looks to the Greek concept of virtue, as well as the "master morality" he describes in *Beyond Good and Evil*. Thus, the camel must metamorphose into the lion who is able to assert its own will and conquer inherited values, although it may not yet be able to create its own.

Oedipus is this lion in the desert. "Thou shalt not kill, thou shalt honor thy mother and father!" speaks the dragon, but Oedipus replies "I will!" and is exalted for it. Oedipus has killed the father and it is this id-like Oedipal spirit that has similarly killed God the father. "God is dead" announces Zarathustra, and it is the Oedipal spirit that is the murderer.

This Oedipal persona, he who has killed the father, is powerful but nonetheless limited. Like the lion of the three metamorphoses, he can slay the dragon of old values but lacks the capability of creating new ones. This deficit derives from the fact that, like the nineteenth century European intellectual climate of Nietzsche's time, *Oedipus cannot face the truth with his eyes open.* Nietzsche's fear for European thought is rooted in the terror of man after the realization that God is dead and that we have killed him. When the metanarrative of scientific truth—another transcendent value system fully launched with the Enlightenment—collapses in a similar fashion, man is destined for *nihilism.* When Oedipus realizes his own truth, he too retreats to the comforting darkness of nihilism by plucking out his eyes. Nietzsche, however, demands that we go further, that we overcome ourselves, that we see the truths and the lies while still opening our eyes to say *Yes* to life. Zarathustra is this child. The hermit who encounters Zarathustra on his descent from the mountain to the world of man (a descent that is reminiscent of the philosopher's return to the cave in Plato's *Republic*) recognizes his awakening, saying: "Zarathustra has changed, Zarathustra has become a child, Zarathustra is an awakened one; what do you now want among the sleepers?"[8] Zarathustra understands and accepts the death of God, but still abides by the wisdom of the earth with an affirming *Yes*. In this he is free for the task of valuation, the task of the child in the final metamorphosis.

The three movements of the spirit can be represented by the progression of Christ, Oedipus and Zarathustra. It is perhaps strange, however, to speak of *progression* when in fact this progression of mythical figures moves *backwards* in time, from Christ at the beginning of the first millennium, to Oedipus in the fifth century B.C., to Zarathustra (derived from the Persian figure Zoroaster) who dates back to two millennia B.C. It would not be consistent with Nietzsche to envision a linear dialectical progression toward some future *Übermensch* (the famed Nietzschean "Superman"), but rather more likely that the metamorphosis of the spirit is something that *goes back to* or *recurs*.

5.

Heidegger wrote a massive work entitled, quite simply, *Nietzsche*. It is an amazing account of what Nietzsche's thought would have been, had Nietzsche been Heidegger. The question is repeatedly put forth: who is Nietzsche's Zarathustra? Heidegger returns us to the notion that Zarathustra is a teacher of the eternal recurrence and a bridge to the *Übermensch*. He inquires into the nature of this bridge.

> Nietzsche has Zarathustra say: "For *that man be redeemed from revenge*—that is for me the bridge to the highest hope and a rainbow after long storms." How strange, how alien these words must seem to the customary view of Nietzsche's philosophy that we have furnished for ourselves. Is not Nietzsche supposed to be the one who goads our will to power, incites us to a politics of violence and war, and sets the "blond beast" on his rampage? The words "that man be

redeemed from revenge" are even italicized in the text. Nietzsche's thought thinks in the direction of redemption from the spirit of revenge. . . . But then why is it that something so decisive depends of redemption from revenge? Where is the spirit of revenge at home? Nietzsche replies to our question in the third-to-last episode of the second part of *Thus Spoke Zarathustra*, which bears the heading "On Redemption." Here the following words appear: "The *spirit of revenge*: my friends, up to now that was man's best reflection; and wherever there was suffering, there also had to be punishment."[9]

Overcoming the spirit of revenge, from one perspective a step from Judaism to Christianity, takes on a more psychological significance here. Christian thought attempted (in principle) to turn us away from the "eye for an eye" sensibilities of Judaism, in order to purge us of a vengeful and punitive attitude toward *others*. It appears as if Nietzsche wishes to cure us of the Christian sensibility that engenders a vengeful and punitive attitude toward *ourselves*. In the context of Nietzsche's thought, the association of punishment with suffering is also part of the Christian legacy. For those of "herd morality," the Christian superego adds insult to injury by associating guilt and causal significance to suffering, rather than viewing it as a part of the human, that is to say natural, condition. Not only must we suffer, but we must punish ourselves for the guilt that has brought this suffering about. Thus in *The Anti-Christ* does Nietzsche praise Buddhism for its "struggle against suffering," as opposed to the Christian "struggle against sin."

6.

But why is *your* redemption better, Nietzsche? How is *your* eternity more eternal? Why is your resurrection and reincarnation any different? What special value does your "truth" have, when you claim that truth is nothing but perspective? What has your son to offer us that the son of God has not already given—and without the contamination of misogyny, anti-Semitism, and proto-Nazism? Would you be such a misogynist if you had fallen asleep on the soft breasts of Salomé rather than on the hard words of Schopenhauer? You said that every man bears with him a picture of woman derived from his mother—what picture do you carry? Have you ever seen the frightening picture I have carried for so many years? And Christ? Could Christ anoint the feet of Magdalene only because his own mother was a virgin? Has your son Zarathustra truly gone beyond Christ, or merely beyond the average Christian? Has he even gone beyond Socrates? Is your eternal recurrence any less metaphysical or otherworldly than the Forms or the Kingdom of Heaven? Have you truly gone beyond Platonism? Or Christianity, your so-called Platonism for the masses? You, a Dionysus? *Christ* turned water into wine and then *you* turned it into piss and vinegar. Did you ever dance, Nietzsche? Did you ever dance naked? Could a sickly, clumsy bookworm like you ever dance? The *anti*-Christ? Holy Christ! You didn't say anything about Christianity that the Marquis de Sade hadn't said a hundred years earlier—and he *lived* his contempt, rather than simply *writing* it.

It has been said that the enlightened monk can spit in the face of the Buddha. Is it now time for me to spit in your face, in the face of all of you arrogant philosophers, and perhaps in the face of philosophy itself? Wittgenstein is almost as intolerable as you. The unmitigated *hubris* to believe he dissolved all problems of philosophy with his measly little *Tractatus*! The entire project reeks of narcissistic entitlement and aristocracy. Only someone who came from a family as wealthy as the Wittgensteins would presume that there is an inherent connection between language and the world, for only the wealthy can alter the world by mere *fiat*. Wittgenstein trimmed logic and language in the same way a persnickety queen trims hair! And you, Hegel, with your grandiose dialectic. When did you come up with that one—while quaffing beer and fucking your sister? You gave us your dialectic as if it were an infinite sponge, soaking up everything in history. But doesn't an infinite sponge require an infinite number of holes?

You have given us your son, Nietzsche—would you sacrifice him also? What does your son have to do with my sins? Who is Zarathustra to me? Who and where is my father? Who will sacrifice me? Tell me! Show yourself, coward! Step from the shadows, rise from the tomb! Make yourself manifest to me as Christ did to *his* disciples! Come, Apostate, to your adoring Apostle! What Apostles are there for the Christ who preaches the golden rule of *no neighbor, no self*? The prancing Apostles of Keynes's Cambridge? We are all Buddhas and Christs, are we not? Who will be my Matthew, Mark, Luke, or John? Who will be my Plato or my Xenophon? Who will record my trial and my death? What will be my Gospels or my Dialogues? Who but me? What but my fragments?

zarathustra must die

1.

He was remarkably calm that day, especially given the controversy swirling around the dissertation. Before one could even depart from the gates of the first page, he had created a stir. The cryptic title inspired the contempt of the large analytic philosophical community at the University and the praise of the Continental romantics—his image seemed to be fragmented between philosophical charlatan and visionary. There was also the matter of its excessive length. A demanding but gifted student, he was forgiven this transgression on his assurance that every page was of essential relevance. It was, however, the nature of this "relevance" that ultimately caused a disturbance. While the vast majority of his thesis was reputed to be cogent, lucid, and original, there were certain . . . irregularities. Friends, faculty, and fellow students were left to their imaginations until excerpts of the work spread through the university like a virus. It came to light that approximately one hundred pages—the final pages of the work—were nearly incomprehensible. Even his many apologists in the Continental tradition were perplexed, or at least silent. Esoteric notes were scribbled in the margins of his final copy. Statements such as "I am the son of Zarathustra" or "My dialectic is the temporal unfolding of eternal analytic truths" garnished the meat of his argumentation. The campus coffeehouse buzz in the weeks preceding his lecture was the question of genius versus gibberish.

The advisor, the committee, the department chair and the administration were confused and conflicted. On the one hand, the work revealed philosophical talent. On the other, the bizarre inclusions suggested at best a maverick and at worst an unstable mind. Revision was initially proposed as an option, but he would not hear of it. "The work is an indivisible whole" he urged with an air of caution, as if splitting off parts would unleash the catastrophic energy of atomic fission. Remarkably, Dorian got his way. The university was cautiously hopeful to claim this young thinker as their own and so deferred judgment until the day of the defense. This, they reasoned, would sufficiently tell the tale.

Such drama did not usually accompany a doctoral dissertation in a field as ostensibly inert as philosophy. In this case, however, the events and discussion leading up to the defense led to a certain electricity, no doubt enhanced by his conspicuous absence in the weeks preceding it. The rumors began to fly and squeak— noisy black bats always welcomed in the Ivory Tower. Some thought he was on vacation, decompressing. Others thought he was beyond decompression and had simply gone insane. One student claimed he was arrested in Germany for exhuming the corpse of Nietzsche.

Many had been following the strange saga and were determined to attend the defense. Faculty members in various departments had rescheduled classes, whereas others had simply canceled. Hearing rumors that the numbers in attendance might very well swell to hundreds, the venue was changed from the Department Library to the old auditorium in Orforde Hall. It was speculated that the change held significance beyond a move to a more accommodating facility. It was well known that this was the room where, in the late 1960s, the legendary doctoral candidate Jay Allen was driven to madness during the defense of his dissertation on Kant. Allen, now a university icon who was already a deeply disturbed genius when he began his PhD, experienced a complete meltdown in the heat of battle about Kant's Transcendental Deduction. "Hiding" under the table in the plain view of hundreds, he rocked backed and forth, singing childhood songs and playing out some weird simulacrum of hide-and-seek. It was speculated that Dorian's committee would exert a pressure intended to test the pervasive hypothesis that he was mentally unstable. History, it was thought, was about to repeat itself.

Orforde Hall was, in a word, venerable. A steep amphitheater, the seats sloped like a mahogany wave poised to roll into a marble beachhead. The stage brightly illuminated, one expected to find nineteenth-century surgeons diligently dissecting a belly or a brain, pausing only to use an ungloved hand to straighten a silk cravat. As one of the first there, he savored the must and the silence. Slowly, they started to trickle in. Seats filled, voices chattered, book-heavy bags dropped hammer-like to the floor. A moldy coat of academics grew over the seats, then the floors, then the hall.

Mostly pencil-necked and pasty-faced, they provoked nothing but contempt in him: the colors of their thought-world were bright only in contrast to the pallid canvas of their life-world.

Birds flying harum-scarum can quite remarkably settle on a tree with a mysterious synchrony. So, too, the reverberant conversations seemed to die off in an instant as the three gowned-and-hooded committee members walked solemnly to the stage and ceremoniously took their seats. Next, the prominent figure of Dr. Hans Regelstein positioned himself, his academic robe ruffling with nervousness. Finally, Dr. Arielle Tempe approached the stage. It was she, traditionally, who would formally introduce the doctoral candidate and end the defense with a final and provocative question. With pawns and queens finally assembled, the audience rose as the game began. Before the crisp edge of the silence could cut, Dr. Tempe—arm extended toward stage left—called out: "I present Mr. Dorian Alexander, who will defend his dissertation 'A Phenomenological De-Distancing of Nietzsche's Doctrine of the Eternal Return,' in partial fulfillment of the requirements for the degree Doctor of Philosophy."

What happened next shocked all who were present—Dorian proceeded with utter lucidity. A concise and comprehensive lecture introduced the problematic of time and eternity from Plato to Einstein, progressed to a more extensive discussion of Nietzsche's doctrine of the eternal return and concluded with his own thesis. He was tempered and polished and while his talk lacked the ability to inflame, it also lacked the ability to inspire. He was neither the madman nor the genius, but rather an intelligent and able doctoral candidate. He answered questions with precision and erudition, drawing on both the analytic and Continental traditions. He was engaging and present—but somehow not Dorian. The committee, who had feared a spectacle, became demonstrably relieved midway through his performance: shoulders relaxed, backs slouched and brows unfurrowed. Pursed lips slowly unfurled and curled in unthreatened interest, as they began their questioning with vigor, but also with measure. There was no confrontation, no challenge, no journey into the center of his strange thinking, but rather a leisurely Sunday drive through the suburbs of his intellect.

The audience became disgruntled—they had come for blood and were given tomato juice. While impressive, it was still within the domain of the ordinary. What was he doing? Years ago, he would have scoffed at this temerity and forced them all to swallow the bitter yet "therapeutic" pill of his thoughts. On this day, however, he seemed to be in collusion, seemed to be one of them. Dorian knew what was at stake—a raving performance would have ended his doctoral program and his career. He had too much savvy to allow that to happen. On the other hand, there seemed to be something deeper. It was as if, suddenly, that the words of philosophy no longer *meant* anything to him. It was as if, suddenly, *that Dorian was dead.*

Over an hour had passed, and a lull in the conversation presented itself. Dr. Tempe rose, signaling that the defense was coming to an end.

"Dr. Alexander," she began, confirming the assumption that he would, indeed, pass, "If you could ask Nietzsche one question right now, what would it be?"

It was only then that he seemed to unravel. There was a pause for some minutes, followed by a discomfort in the crowd. *Dorian fell into a trance and softly smiled.* The pause became pregnant and after a brief gestation it gave birth to a silence. *His eyes closed and his face contorted.* The silence created an unease, which subsequently transformed to a frustration. *He wept.* The frustration broke down to an exhaustion and cleared the way for a calm. *He was finally at peace.* And in that peace, in which time seemed to expand to an infinite moment, Dorian took a breath and softly replied.

2.

"If you could ask Nietzsche one question right now, what would it be?"

There was a pause for some minutes, followed by a discomfort in the crowd. I fell into a trance. Slowly I drifted downward and softly smiled, for I was falling again to the corals.

Soon, my stomach started to sour and my head began to swell. I was accelerating, free falling. Open my eyes to see sunlight . . . *not* in water . . . but in *air* . . . Going down . . . to mountain not coral . . . See far into distance below . . . terrified . . . Sea and land and mountain . . . the corals below? . . . No—no corals . . . Women . . . Not corals? but women? . . . mother? . . . Each with a dozen outstretched arms . . . and spinning . . . on a mountain . . . Festival . . . music and shrill screams . . . Figures on the ground . . . being pulled and tugged from down under . . . Flickering clips . . . falling faster . . . in fear . . . Brain exploding with pulse . . . stomach sour . . . Swirling vortex . . . Event horizon . . . Going to die . . . Past gone . . . no future . . . I sorry . . . want forgiveness . . . want to forgive . . . want to love . . . want . . . Getting hotter, falling faster . . . simply want . . . Going to die . . . Ground approaching . . . Simply want . . . Going to die . . . Simply want . . . to say . . . *Yes!* . . .

A shock running through me, I jump awake. This is not, however, the jump that narrowly precedes the impact of a dream fall, for the fall was no dream. Am I going insane? The mountain is black, porous, warm, and the naked women are teeming over it like insects. They are in ecstasy, spinning and screaming in abandon. And arms: all over them, all over each other, all over the mountain. Arms reaching out for wine, for bread, for each other. They caress themselves with two hands and caress their neighbor with three more. Octopus upon octopus stroking each other, moaning, murmuring in a tongue I cannot understand. Teeming over the mountain, teeming over each other, they are wet and sticky with saliva and wine and blood. They scream and the crater groans in answer, belching sulfurous yellow smoke high into the air. I cannot move, feel the ground vibrating. Shrill screams, synchronous, blade shredding air and space. Some arms interlocking, still more flailing in air, still more on breasts, still more in vaginas. Eyes only white, they scream. Nearly unbearable, nearly unbearable. More arms interlocking, dancing, flesh Medusa grabbing flesh Medusa, now a centipede dancing, leaning in and back, rotating around the crater, centipede becoming millipede, shrill becoming shriller, tremors turn to quake as the volcano swells, they surround the crater and scream, voices mingling in the abyss, nearly unbearable, nearly unbearable, circling they scream, many voices become one, hovers over the crater, treble rolls down to bass, roils low, and suddenly I hear! I understand! They are calling! They are calling for him! They are calling for Dionysus! They scream out—*Apollo must die!* Greece! Lands are falling around the mountain! The Aegis is sinking! *The Aegis is sinking!* They lean over the crater, their mouths are open, they await the eruption! The earth is falling into the water! Dionysus is coming! Apollo must die! Apollo must die! I am falling again! Black earth opening up! Hot ejaculation of molten orange! The coming of fire high into the atmosphere! They bathe in the flames of Dionysus! Their arms are burning, flesh falling hot wax! Flesh melted, revealing sharp steel bones! Arms, voices, blades! Flesh Medusas heave themselves into the crater! Steely-armed women spinning like fans and helicopters! One jumps over me in abortive flight!

I awake with a start, but again, this is no dream. The air reeks of sulfur and soot. I am surrounded by a sorority of warriors, with sword arms clinking and chinking against each other. They are bloodied and I know the myth—sacrifices have been made. They encircle me, methodically, in synchrony, in ritual. Leaning in, leaning back. Leaning in, leaning back. They are calling out, some litany, some chant, some chorus. They are calling out and again I hear! I understand!

"Christ must die!"

The camel falls from the sky, nostrils flaring, and turns to me with eyes of angst and brute supplication. They pounce and the water from its impaled humps shoots forth, pouring over us, evaporating on the hot rocks. The atmosphere is thick with steam and smoke and *I cannot breathe.* The camel snorts and groans, writhes in mindless animal agony, its limbs outstretched as it is feasted upon.

Again, the chant begins and I hear! I understand!

"Oedipus must die!"

The lion appears, growling fiercer than the mountain, brandishing the sword of "I will!"—but to no avail. They attack with blade and flame, rending it into clumps of hair and seared flesh. Its blood shoots forth, pouring over us, becoming a hot wet paste covering the rocks. They circle again. The bowels of the mountain shake, releasing flatus of sulfur. Again they scream. Unbearable, unbearable.

"Zarathustra must die! ZARATHUSTRA MUST DIE!"

For all of the unworldly sights, I cannot believe my eyes. The millipede of flesh and steel dismembers, and the Maenads silently, almost reverently look down the mountain. Only footsteps can be heard as a cool twilight suddenly falls. Below, hobbling up to the peak is none other than the wanderer and his shadow. Eyes squinting and bespectacled, squirrel-tail mustache nearly white, he appears aged and infirm. *Nietzsche.*

Slowly, feebly he climbs, the beautiful flesh of Zarathustra held tightly in his arm. His pride, his joy, his greatest gift. His only son, about to be sacrificed in a festival of Dionysus: the scene is pure, unadulterated Nietzschean irony. Nietzsche, not the young Christ walking to Golgotha, but the old Jew, the new Abraham climbing to the top of the high mountain of philosophy to sacrifice his Isaac. Did Nietzsche not have a covenant? Was not Zarathustra to give birth to clans and tribes? What command was Nietzsche about to follow? The command of irony? Or of *women*? The old misogynist—he hated them because he knew they held in their sole possession what he desperately craved . . . true power. I would not let him falter, would not let the young creator of values be slain, for I would be the ram in the thistle.

"No! Take me!"

And they hear! They understand!

"Ecce Homo! Let the son of Zarathustra die!"

They turn, they circle, they dance, they chant. They understand and accept the new sacrifice. My eyes close and my face contorts as I anticipate my fate, the fate of Pentheus, the fate of all men who desire to have their heads severed from their hearts, who wish to ignore the wisdom of the feminine, the feminine that can give birth to something real.

Again, I awake. This is no dream. I am staring at my body.

Staring. At my body. Staring at my vessels pumping bright red blood from the severed stump of my neck. Somehow, it too recognizes me. Its arms awkwardly reach out, it clumsily tries to stand, but falls senselessly. I feel, I feel . . . I feel very little, but suddenly start to see. I see the space in between, the Cartesian matrix and Cartesian duality, the *res cogitans* and *res extensa* cut off from one another. I see the space, see the gap into which men disappear, see the disembodied head of the bath house, see the talking heads of New York, see my father's head weeping, see my mother's head in the noose, as I found her swinging from the rafters so many years ago. I see the anesthetic insulation of my intellect from my emotion, see the hiding place in between, see the space to which we retreat when we cannot become what we are. I see the space of disconnection, the space of *my* disconnection. *I see the space called time.* Time, the hiding place of the frightened, the storage bin of unwanted emotions, the shadow of true life, the asylum from the discomforting burden of eternity. I see the space called time and I weep. I weep for my sins and for my being sundered. I weep for the clumsy body that writhes in stupidity before me, the rubbery flesh exsanguinating before my very eyes. I weep and I remember, I return and I love, I yearn and I forgive. *I forgive! I forgive others . . . I forgive myself! I want to live, want simply to be in each moment! I desire everything and everyone, just as it is, just as they are! Love and indifference, disease and joy, the sublime and the banal, I want it all! Everything from my thought to my feces! It is all me! It must be all me and I forgive! And I love! And if I do not love, then I give myself license to hate! I want to say* Yes *to life, even when it means saying* No*! I crave each moment, whatever it brings, I crave to look at each moment and know: thus have I willed it, thus must it be! No fantasy, no past, no time! I long for the eternal, I long to say* YES!

Again, I awake. I feel the hands of a man gently holding my face. Night has fallen and I see little but the faint reflection of glasses. *Is it him?*

"Dorian . . . " he whispers slowly *"Werde was Du bist. Become what you are!"*

Become what I am. Have the courage to cross the abyss of time, to let each self within me speak, fight, *scream*! Yes, become what I am! Have the strength not to elide the conflicts of the many selves with a grand narrative, nor let them sit as isolated canvases in the museum, nor let them rest comfortably in a compromising consensus. No, become what I am! Lean into the conflict, lean into the tension, let the space called time finally break down to the eternal. Lean into the struggle, lean into the gathering force until the space no longer insulates but rather conducts the lightning of my self! What did Nietzsche do when the fire finally shot across the sky? *Nietzsche went insane.*

To say *Yes* to each emotion, to struggle toward the eternal, to resist the refuge of time, to comprehend the strange interplay of the self that always is and the self that must be brought into being, to engage in that bizarre process and that mysterious state called becoming what one is, only this will give me the courage to approach each moment as if it were to recur forever. Only this will give me the courage to approach each moment as if it were to occur *only once.*

I was quietly joyful when again I felt the beating of my heart and the familiar *whoosh-whoosh* of blood pulsing into my brain. I was finally at peace. And in that peace, in which time seemed to expand to an infinite moment, I took a breath and softly replied.

"Sweet Jesus, Nietzsche—why *are* you so wise?"

Endnotes

1. Friedrich Nietzsche, *Beyond Good and Evil*, aphorism 75, page 271, in *Basic Writings of Nietzsche*, translated by Walter Kaufman, Modern Library: New York.

2. Friedrich Nietzsche, *Ecce Homo*, page 674, in *Basic Writings of Nietzsche*, translated by Walter Kaufman, Modern Library: New York.

3. Friedrich Nietzsche, *Beyond Good and Evil*, aphorism 108, page 275, in *Basic Writings of Nietzsche*, translated by Walter Kaufman, Modern Library: New York.

4. Friedrich Nietzsche, *Beyond Good and Evil*, aphorism 139, page 278, in *Basic Writings of Nietzsche*, translated by Walter Kaufman, Modern Library: New York.

5. Friedrich Nietzsche, *The Gay Science*, aphorism 341, Vantage Books: New York.

6. Friedrich Nietzsche, *Human, All Too Human*, aphorism 384, page 150, translated by R.J. Hollingdale, Cambridge University Press: Cambridge.

7. Friedrich Nietzsche, *Beyond Good and Evil*, aphorism 117, page 276, in *Basic Writings of Nietzsche*, translated by Walter Kaufman, Modern Library: New York.

8. Friedrich Nietzsche, *Thus Spoke Zarathustra*, page 11, translated by Walter Kaufmann, Penguin Books: New York.

9. Martin Heidegger, *Nietzsche* (Volume 2, paperback edition), page 219, translated by David Farrell Krell, Harper: San Francisco (Harper Collins).

Books from Etruscan Press

The Disappearance of Seth | Kazim Ali
Drift Ice | Jennifer Atkinson
Crow Man | Tom Bailey
Coronology | Claire Bateman
Cinder | Bruce Bond
Peal | Bruce Bond
Toucans in the Arctic | Scott Coffel
Body of a Dancer | Renée E. D'Aoust
Nahoonkara | Peter Grandbois
Confessions of Doc Williams & Other Poems | William Heyen
A Poetics of Hiroshima | William Heyen
Shoah Train | William Heyen
September 11, 2001, American Writers Respond | Edited by William Heyen
As Easy As Lying | H. L. Hix
Chromatic | H. L. Hix
First Fire, Then Birds | H. L. Hix
God Bless | H. L. Hix
Incident Light | H. L. Hix
Legible Heavens | II. L. Hix
Lines of Inquiry | H. L. Hix
Shadows of Houses | H. L. Hix
Wild and Whirling Words: A Poetic Conversation | H. L. Hix
Art Into Life | Frederick R. Karl
Free Concert: New and Selected Poems | Milton Kessler
Parallel Lives | Michael Lind
The Burning House | Paul Lisicky
Synergos | Robert Manzano
The Gambler's Nephew | Jack Matthews
Venison | Thorpe Moeckel
So Late, So Soon | Carol Moldaw
The Widening | Carol Moldaw
Saint Joe's Passion | JD Schraffenberger
Lies Will Take You Somewhere | Sheila Schwartz
Fast Animal | Tim Seibles
American Fugue | Alexis Stamatis
The Casanova Chronicles | Myrna Stone
White Horse: A Columbian Journey | Diane Thiel
The Fugitive Self | John Wheatcroft

Etruscan Is Proud of Support Received From

Wilkes University

Youngstown State University

The Raymond John Wean Foundation

The Ohio Arts Council

The Stephen & Jeryl Oristaglio Foundation

The Nathalie & James Andrews Foundation

The National Endowment for the Arts

The Ruth H. Beecher Foundation

The Bates-Manzano Fund

The New Mexico Community Foundation

Founded in 2001 with a generous grant from the Oristaglio Foundation, Etruscan Press is a nonprofit cooperative of poets and writers working to produce and promote books that nurture the dialogue among genres, achieve a distinctive voice, and reshape the literary and cultural histories of which we are a part.

etruscan press
www.etruscanpress.org

Etruscan Press books may be ordered from

Consortium Book Sales and Distribution
800.283.3572
www.cbsd.com

Small Press Distribution
800.869.7553
www.spdbooks.com

Etruscan Press is a 501(c)(3) nonprofit organization.
Contributions to Etruscan Press are tax deductible
as allowed under applicable law.
For more information, a prospectus,
or to order one of our titles,
contact us at books@etruscanpress.org.